LOVE'S BODY CHECK

THE CAROLINA HOCKEY SERIES - BOOK 1

JOSIE NACLERIO

ROMANCE FOR THE AGES PUBLISHING

Love's Body Check – The Carolina Hockey Series – Book 1 – 1st Edition © Copyright 2023 by Josie Naclerio.

Published in the United States of America. First published in February 2023

Romance for the Ages Publishing

ISBN: 9798375414355

Cover Design: Tracie Douglas at Dark Water Covers

Team Logo Design: Tracie Douglas at Dark Water Covers

Photos Courtesy: J Michael Walker Photography and Deposit Photos

coincidental. If I used any name inadvertently, please understand it is purely unintentional.

For more information, contact the author at josienaclerioauthor@gmail.com or on Facebook: Josie Naclerio – Author.

Warning: This book may contain offensive language, violence, adult, and sexual situations. Mature audiences only, 18+ years of age. Not appropriate for younger or trigger-sensitive audiences. Read at your own risk.

✽ Created with Vellum

DEDICATION

This book is dedicated to my good friend and fellow Bruin's fanatic, Brandy Novak- Dixon. Her courage and strength in overcoming a life of addiction and becoming something more than another statistic laid the foundation for Seth's past. Brandy hasn't forgotten her struggles but utilizes them to help current addicts find the road to recovery and maintaining an addiction-free life. This book is also for all those still addicted and those that continue the daily struggle to remain drug free. As with any addiction, recovery requires a lifetime of struggles and continual support.

ACKNOWLEDGMENTS

I'd like to extend a thank you to my hockey friends. Each has helped bring a personal, first-hand authenticity to my characters. Your eagerness and willingness to answer questions is appreciated. I hope my characters reflect your valued input.

Parker Milner retired pro hockey player and former South Carolina Stingray. A self-proclaimed foodie and current food editor for Charleston's Post and Courier.

Nate Pionk, pro hockey player and former South Carolina Stingray. Pionk's Posse will live on. Remember what the lawman said, "Wanted dead or alive."

David Seitz retired pro hockey player and former South Carolina Stingray.

Greg DiTomaso, pro hockey player and former South Carolina Stingray, my social media blurb model.

Travis Ward, our South Carolina Stingrays equipment manager.

Mario Picciotto of the South Carolina Stingrays. Your help navigating intricacies of the NHL, AHL, and ECHL contracts, waivers, and players moving between the leagues.

Colin Vokey, my medical advisor, for the hours of your time, knowledge and helping with the various injury and medical scenes.

Jenny Castle Turner, my Boston Bruins friend, for helping me with a specific scene.

Rob Gutro, my good friend, fellow author, and medium, for your help with editing and keeping me motivated and always supporting my writing.

Carolyn Dasen-Hoxworth (my supportive aunt) and Megan Ross

(fellow Stingrays fan and friend), for being my BETA readers and helping with the editing and proofreading.

M.K. Collins, your help with fine-tuning the blurb for this book is greatly appreciated.

Rebecca Norman, again a huge, special thanks for your hours of help with plotting, editing, character development, and keeping me inspired and motivated. Your friendship is a blessing. She writes wonderful Regency era books and an awesome ancient Roman/modern mix series that are some of my favorites written under Rosie Chapel.

Tracie Douglas at Dark Water Covers, for producing eye-catching covers and setting me on the path of 'branding' this series and the future hockey series books and designing the Charleston Patriots hockey team logo. Tracie also offers formatting services.

Kimberly L. Baker, my proofreader. Wow, you catch so much stuff I miss, and helping me to grow and improve as a writer.

Also, an extra thank you to all my police and hockey family and my wonderful community of Edisto Beach for your continued encouragement and support this past year as I battled a third back injury requiring surgery.

Thank you to my Stingrays ladies, Sonia, Kelly, Glenna, and Nicole, who I enjoy hanging out with by the glass watching our boys during warm-ups. More scenes and characters have developed from those twenty minutes than you know.

Thank you to all my readers, followers, friends, and family who continue encouraging me to keep writing. These books are for you.

Special thanks to my wonderful, patient, and supportive husband, Ken, who also plays the role of my law enforcement advisor.

LOVE'S BODY CHECK

the Carolina Hockey Series

JOSIE NACLERIO

CHAPTER 1

Twenty-one-year-old Seth Doyle laced his battered skates. One snapped and he cursed. He concentrated on his task but maintained a vigilant awareness of the other guys in the locker room. A rare pang of inhibition stabbed him. His equipment and uniform's condition tiers below the others, prompting a moment of misgiving, but he shrugged it off.

Seth hadn't survived living on the intercity streets of Chicago this long feeling sorry for himself or envying what others had. His belief he might someday escape the city and turn his life around dwindled each passing day.

He reduced his meals to once a day, helping save money. The warmer summer months proved less of a challenge finding adequate sleeping accommodations. He currently had a roof over his head until his welcome wore out. The agreement provided a rent-free, warm, semi-safe residence.

A breath drawn in, he stood, picked up his heavily taped and repaired stick, and headed to the ice. New skates and a stick did him no good if he was dead.

Warm-ups completed, the group of men, aged in their thirties with a handful of older guys, gathered at center ice. Seth the youngest. His confidence increased. He'd skate rings around these guys.

The captains selecting players, each new round bypassed Seth. Years of fending for himself enabled him to keep his expression neutral, but the slight fed the demon of self-doubt badgering him and undermining his confidence in his hockey skills.

He found himself playing for the gold team by default, and experiencing a pang of sadness at the slight, but remaining undeterred. Seth hadn't traveled here via a convoluted series of buses and a three-mile walk to let his insecurities override his long-held dream of skating with his idol.

MARSHALL REEVES PAID scant attention to the new kid suiting up in the locker room, other than noting his mismatched uniform and battered, piecemeal equipment.

The young defenseman skating circles around him and the others intrigued him. A memory of a group of kids he encountered one night in Englewood on his way home from a community policing meeting jumped into his mind, but he pushed it aside and concentrated on the game.

Marshall participated in the pick-up games during the summer months for the sheer joy of skating, playing, and keeping in shape. He spent the rest of the year focused on developing Boston's prospects and ensuring each player progressed from their East Coast Hockey League affiliate, the Charleston Patriots, to their American Hockey League team and on to their ultimate destination, the National Hockey League.

Players came and went in the ECHL, but no defenseman exhibited the raw talent of this kid.

Back on the ice for his next shift, Marshall committed an unaccustomed mistake and dipped his head on the play unfolding...and found himself sprawled on the ice.

. . .

SETH'S PREDICTION regarding his skating abilities compared to the others proved fruitful. On this line change, Seth pounced on Marshall's mistake. His idol knocked to the ice, he snagged the loose puck, but three opponents swarmed him. A barrage of shouting, pushing, and shoving ensued, and Seth responded.

Fists flew until others hauled him away from his attackers.

The player who punched Seth in the mouth, pointed at Seth first and then Marshall. "What the hell is wrong with you? It's a fucking pickup game, asshole. He's Marshall Reeves, you idiot."

Seth glanced at Marshall levering himself to his feet.

"Yeah. So, what. He knows to keep his head up."

One of Marshall's teammates leapt at Seth a second time and unleashed a barrage of insults. Seth spat a slew of chirps, hockey lingo for trash talking, in return.

This time, several of Seth's punches hit their mark, until the others broke them apart.

"Leave. We don't want your kind of play here," the opposition's team captain said.

"Yeah, fine. Whatever." Seth shoved the two men blocking his path and skated away.

"Let him stay. The hit was legal, and he's right, I know better."

"Marshall, we—"

He ignored the others.

"Hey, kid. What's your name?".

Seth stopped in his tracks.

"Marshall. Let him go," His teammate said.

"Shut up, Hank. The kid is good, real, good. He's skating circles around everyone, me included." Marshall skated away from the group and toward Seth.

Seth's face unreadable.

"What's your name?" Marshall repeated.

"Seth."

"Last name." He studied the younger man, noting his hardened appearance hid his youth.

"Doyle."

"Where are you playing?"

"Here tonight." Seth hated himself for the vague answer.

"How old are you?" Marshall eyed the tall youngster. His evasive answers spiking his curiosity.

"Kind of a personal question." The hint of a smile tugged at Seth's mouth.

"I'm guessing twenty-three."

"Twenty-one."

Marshall chuckled at Seth's correction.

"Hey, Marshall, are we playing or what?" one of the guys asked.

"We're playing." Marshall smiled at Seth and patted his shoulder. "Come on kid."

"We're trading Doyle for Sampson." Marshall pointed to the defenseman on his team.

"Wait, we don't do—"

"We do now." Marshall's expression halted further objections, and the changes made, play resumed.

SETH USED extra care loosening his tattered skate laces. Changed into regular clothes, he pulled on his sneakers and paused. His eyes ran the length of the individual standing in front of him.

Marshall Reeves.

"We're going for brews and food, join us."

"Thanks. I work early in the morning." Seth hedged. He did work in the morning, but his immediate concern was lack of transportation. If he missed the last bus, he'd be hoofing it all the way home to the other side of the city.

"You never answered my question about where you're playing."

"Uh, yeah, well—"

"Reeves. See you and the kid at The Grill."

"No saying no now, kid." Marshall smiled.

"I can't go." Seth rose from the bench and gathered his gear. Embarrassment a new emotion for him and he hurried away.

"Seth. Doyle." Marshall's gaze lingered on the younger man's back.

Seth pushed open the exit door and quickened his pace.

Marshall chased after Seth. He exited the building and scanned the parking lot. The youngster nowhere around, he exhaled his frustration, and climbed into his SUV. He cranked the engine and the headlights illuminating the lot and street, Marshall spied a figure, a hockey bag slung across his shoulder, walking on the darkened side of the road and he drove in that direction.

"What the…" Marshall lowered the Cayenne's window.

"Seth. What are you doing?"

"Going home. I work in the morning."

"Why the hell are you walking? Where is home?" Marshall demanded, positioning his vehicle alongside Seth, and matching his pace.

Seth ignored him. He halted once Marshall maneuvered his Cayenne in front of him.

Marshall stepped out of the SUV, and said, "You don't speak much, do you?"

"Nothing to say."

"Get in I'll drive you home."

Seth's silence prompted Marshall into rounding the vehicle and blocking Seth from skirting around the SUV.

"Get in the car, Doyle."

Marshall opened the Cayenne's cargo hatch, and Seth stashed his gear inside. Outside the front passenger side door, Seth, in an unconscious gesture brushed at his pants and climbed in.

"Nice ride."

"Thanks."

Seth finished towel drying his hair, dressed, and entered the bedroom Marshall directed him to use. A knock on the door startling him, he gathered his composure and said, "Come in."

Lauren Reeves, Marshall's wife, stepped inside, and he mustered a smile.

"Other than you're taller than Marshall, hopefully these fit." Lauren handed him a t-shirt and a pair of athletic shorts.

"Thank you."

"You're welcome. Sleep well, Seth. Good night."

"Good night, Mrs. Reeves."

"Please, it's Lauren."

Seth loitered in the doorway once Lauren left. The giggling coming from down the hall struck a chord. He closed the door and leaned against it.

He avoided dwelling on the what ifs, but tonight he found himself peppered with them. Seth sucked in a breath, pushed away from the door, and changed into the clothing Lauren left.

Stretched out on the bed, he flipped through the numerous television channels, stopping on the NHL Network. Five minutes into the show, he drifted asleep.

"What's his story?" Lauren asked Marshall.

"I don't know. He wouldn't answer any direct questions, but he skates like a son of a bitch." Marshall eyed Lauren sitting alongside him on the bed.

"So, now what?"

"I don't know, Lauren. I should've asked you first."

"Marshall Reeves." Lauren repositioned herself, sitting cross-legged and facing him. "The boy was walking to God knows where and at night. I'll bet he doesn't have a permanent or stable home. You did the right thing."

"I need to make a call." Marshall reached for his cellphone on the nightstand.

Lauren smiled, kissed Marshall, and snuggled beneath the covers, pounding her pillow a few times.

"He'll kill you."

"Yup." Marshall grinned at Lauren. "Hey, Coop."

First, he conversed with Cooper Mills, Charleston's general manager and co-owner of the Patriots. His next conversation with Boston's general manager, Lou Gwynn, was longer. Lou suggested including the team owner, Patrick Hawks.

"You're a glutton for punishment, Marshall."

"Yeah, but…"

"It's late, go to sleep."

CHAPTER 2

No stranger to waking in unfamiliar or unusual places, Seth stretched and glanced around. This room was the nicest he'd ever slept in, and he basked in the comfort of the bed until his internal alarm clock buzzed. A cellphone or watch unaffordable, he learned early on to determine time without the convenience of devices.

He indulged in another luxuriating shower, dressed, and folded the borrowed clothing and placed them on the edge of the bed. Seth paused in the bedroom doorway. He examined the room one last time and released a breath.

Real life called.

At the bottom of the stairs, Seth hesitated, unsure where to go he followed the voices of Marshall and Lauren's two children and entered the kitchen.

"Morning."

"Good morning. Are you hungry? Coffee?" Lauren pointed a cup at the freshly brewed pot.

"I'm good, thank you."

"Never skip a meal, Doyle." Marshall's tone brooked no argument.

"Uh, ok."

"Eggs, bacon, and biscuits, okay?" Lauren smiled, and within seconds, handed Seth a plate heaped with food.

"Thank you." Seth carried the plate to the table.

"Sit next to me," Quintin Reeves said.

"No, he's sitting next to me." Hope shot her brother a challenging glare.

"He doesn't want to sit by a girl."

"You're a real butt ho—"

"Enough." Marshall's raised voice halted his kids' banter.

"How about I sit between both of you." Seth smiled. The suggestion resulting in an immediate seat shuffle and both children pulled him into conversation.

Lauren's eyes meeting her husband's, she smiled.

SETH STUDIED the scenery streaking past the Porsche's window. He braced himself for a barrage of questions, but none came other than asking for his work address.

Marshall turning into the parking lot of Mike's Auto Repair Shop, tension gripped Seth. He dared a glance Marshall's way.

The powerful engine of the expensive SUV idling, garnering his co-workers and boss's attention, Seth placed his hand on the door handle.

Marshall's words halted his exit.

"I've arranged a tryout with our team. I leave for South Carolina in two days. I can't promise anything, but—"

"I'll have to ask if I can leave."

"Give your notice."

"Uh, not the job...my...uh...probation officer."

"Dare I ask for what?"

"Minor possession...I..."

"Go ahead." Marshall regarded Seth, his tone even.

"I don't do hard drugs anymore. I mean, I smoke joints, sometimes, but nothing else, and I haven't smoked one in a month." Seth admitted, without flinching.

"Who's your PO? Was it pot?"

Seth divulged his probation officer's name and nodded.

"I'll talk to him. What time are you off? We'll collect your stuff together."

"Why are you doing this? Why do you give a fuck?"

"If I need to answer that, we'll part company right now and you can kiss a career in the NHL goodbye. Do you *want* to spend your life working on cars, scrapping for food, and finding shelter every night. Being on probation requires having a residence, but I'm guessing wherever you're holed up is temporary." Marshall kept eye contact with Seth.

"Englewood Terrace Apartments. I…uh…"

"Are there any little Doyles running around?"

"No. I better get my stuff and go. He docks an hour if you're late by a minute," Seth said and exited the vehicle.

"What time?" Marshall called through his open window.

"Five-thirty."

"I'll be here. Leave the gear."

"Thanks."

"Coach," Marshall said.

"Thanks, Coach."

ONCE SETH DISAPPEARED inside one of the garage bays, Marshall acknowledged the older, unkempt shop owner.

The Cayenne in drive, Marshall shook his head.

Last season he acquired Tyler Brennan, now Seth Doyle. He straightened out Brennan, and he vowed succeeding with Doyle too.

A BLACK GMC Denali cruising into the repair shop's parking lot caught Seth's attention and he cursed. He didn't bother wiping the grease from his hands or replacing the wrench in the tool chest.

Seth strolled out of the garage bay and scowled at the man exiting the pimped-out SUV.

Tremaine Kingston.

"What are you doing here?"

"Where'd you plant your ass last night? You left clients waiting."

"That's none of your business, and I told you, I'm done."

"You're done when *I* say you're done. You're mine, and I own you. I'll always own you." Tremaine approached Seth, four of his heavies flanking him. One standing on each side, one behind, and the fourth walked behind Seth.

"Not anymore."

Tremaine's smile dropped, his jaw tightened, and he stepped into Seth, their chests touching. He grabbed Seth's face and their eyes riveted on each other. "*No* one, says no to me, Seth. *No one.*"

Seth freed himself from Tremaine's hold and stood his ground. Neither Kingston nor his thugs intimidated him.

"Doyle, chitchat on your own time." The shop owner waved a dirty rag.

"Shut up, old man. We're discussing business." Tremaine glowered. A nod and one of the gangster's prevented the owner from leaving his office.

"Your beef is with me, Tre."

"I don't like your attitude, Seth. Maybe it needs adjusting." Tremaine pulled a gun from his waistband and whipped the barrel into Seth's mouth.

"Go ahead, kill me." Blood dripping from his lacerated lower lip, Seth shouldered past the thug and strode back to the work bays.

Tremaine's mouth opened then shut.

"It's time you and your *friends* left." The shop owner eased a shotgun from behind him.

Tremaine's gaze swung between the shop owner and Seth's back.

"This isn't over, Seth. You're mine, and always will be. No one leaves except in a body bag. Including you. We'll finish this later."

Seth ignored the threat and retreated to the garage bay. Tremaine's penetrating gaze burning holes in his back, Seth swiped his bloodied mouth on his shoulder.

TREMAINE CLIMBED INTO THE SUV, vowing to make Seth pay for his continued disrespect, defiance, and refusal to service his clients, costing him a lot of lost revenue.

SETH STAYED extra vigilant throughout the day. His gut warned him, his time on earth was running out. Escape from Chicago now became imperative or else he'd end up on a cold slab at the morgue and buried in a common grave. Now having turned twenty-one, and a month left on his probation, the opportunity to re-apply for his driver's license inched closer.

Marshall's news this morning sparked a frayed ray of hope of escaping this hell. His sole intent last night, a simple one, skate on the same ice with his idol.

The prospect of leaving the city now imminent, he found himself counting down the time until the end of the day but steeled himself for the possibility of Marshall reneging on his earlier promise.

Seth checked the wall clock, eleven thirty. Six more hours. He had to stay alive for six long hours. He expected a return visit from Tremaine's thugs and his anxiety heightened each passing minute.

A hint of tenderness persisting in his ribs from the last beating a month ago, a daily reminder of how many times he endured 'street talks'. His swollen and cut lip a minor injury compared to what he endured in the past. During the last one he managed fighting back. His secret trips to a boxing gym in the South Side paid off and the new skills saved him from certain death.

His survival drove a deeper wedge between him and Tremaine, and precipitated Seth's need to finding a way to leave this city, and soon.

MARSHALL SIGNED in with the receptionist at the parole and probation department's offices for the Englewood area of Chicago. He knocked on the door of Seth's probation officer and entered upon the summons.

"Reeves, it's been a long time." The officer rose from his desk and extended his hand.

"It has. Can't say I missed any of this."

"Dare I ask why you're interested in Seth Doyle."

"Have you seen this kid skate?" Marshall said, eyeing the probation officer.

"Nope, but I know he played hockey at your community center."

"I arranged for a try out with my team in Charleston, so what do we need to do to get his probation transferred to South Carolina."

"Look, Reeves, I've dealt with hundreds of these kids. Seth Doyle is no different from the others. You're wasting your time."

"He told me he's on for minor possession for pot."

"That's it?"

"Is there more?"

"He's had more than one possession charge, nor is it his first prostitution charge. He shoots heroin and drops Fen, that I know of. His tests have been clean but..." the officer paused, waiting for Marshall's comments, but he stayed silent.

"The kid's been popped numerous times for minor offenses. He's a member of the area's top drug dealing gang, the Kingstonians. Doyle is one of Tremaine Kingston's homeless street kid projects, as he calls them. He turns them into mules, junkies, and pimps them out."

"Is that all?"

"There's no conclusive evidence, but he is the prime suspect in the death of a girl who OD'd. From what the street sources said, Doyle serviced her the night she died, and he was higher than a kite."

"When?"

"Let me check his record." The probation officer opened a manila folder and thumbed through it. "Eighteen months ago. Case is still open."

"Did the autopsy report state her COD was an overdose?"

"It's listed as a possible cause along with strangulation. It noted a ton of bruises. Our guess is the sex got rough. Doyle was high. Once he was coherent, he claimed he knew nothing other than having sex with her and getting high. Our sources said she was into kinky shit."

Marshall absorbed the information and calculated Seth's age at the time of the incident, replying, "When was his last drug test? Anything you can share on his juvie criminal activity."

"Last week." The officer locked his hands behind his head. "And nope, other than street rumors and what he's told me."

"Thanks. I appreciate your time, and the info." Marshall rose and the two shook hands.

"He's trouble, Reeves. I can make further inquiries. Just say the word."

"Does he have a driver's...yeah. Revoked or suspended?"

"Suspended.," the probation officer replied. The two spoke another ten minutes and he said, "I'll get the paperwork taken care of and let you know."

Marshall conveyed his thanks and left the office and building.

Inside his vehicle, Marshall called his childhood best friend, Tony Dryden, the man responsible for saving him from his dark drunken state after he left hockey. He followed Tony's advice and became a Chicago police officer.

The two met for lunch, talking until Marshall's other commitments called.

CHAPTER 3

Marshall arrived at Seth's work a few minutes past four. The shop owner approached his SUV, and he powered down the window and greeted the man.

"He's a good kid. Just needs a chance and proper guidance, and to get out of this hell hole. He's a hard worker."

"I'm giving him a chance, but it's his choice. Tell me everything you know about him."

The man slow to answer, Marshall retrieved his wallet, and waved a fifty-dollar bill.

"Not much. Can't say I've seen him do any hard stuff, but I know he has. He does smoke weed and trades sexual favors for a dry sleeping place and he's in Tremaine Kingston's pocket. Thugs came sniffing around this morning. There's a bad rift between them." The man's eyes slid past Marshall's SUV.

"He's a loner. When he talks, it's hockey. He loves it. Damn kid cut out early yesterday and hopped the buses and walked to a damn rink in the suburbs across town to play in a pickup game last night. Said a former hockey player, his idol, would be playing there…wait." The owner's mouth dropped open.

"What about the girl who overdosed?" Marshall ignored the man's amazement.

"Oh, that, yeah, I've no idea how she croaked. Word on the street is it was from too much partying. Seth knows, he was there. Look, underneath he's a good kid. He works harder than any of the other junkies and losers I have working for me. So, where are you taking him?"

"Away from here. We're leaving now. Seth!" Marshall handed off the money, his gaze stayed riveted on the shop until Seth emerged.

The man trudged away, stopped, and turned. "If he comes back here, he's dead."

"Yeah, I know." Marshall waved the man away and the proprietor scurried off.

Marshall urged Seth inside the Cayenne. His young protégé seated, he put the vehicle in drive and left the intercity of Chicago. He opted taking a longer roundabout route to Winnetka and home.

"Want to tell me about that?" Marshall pointed at Seth's mouth.

"It's nothing."

Marshall waited for further explanation. None came.

"Why didn't you tell me about the other charges?" Marshall asked once he parked the car in the garage.

Seth said nothing.

"You knew I'd find out."

Silence.

"Seth, I'm not holding it against you, but I want honesty from you. You have no hockey history and it'll raise questions—"

"Then why bother with me? Sorry, I didn't play organized hockey and don't have a privileged past. Kind of hard when you live on the streets. I played at your community center, but I aged out. Colleges and pro scouts don't go there looking for prospects. You have no idea how many of those kids playing there, dream of going to college and escaping." His jaw muscle twitched.

Seth's words hit Marshall. "No, you're right. They don't have the same opportunities to achieve their dreams. Maybe we can change that."

"Why? They'll say it's a waste of their time. Those kids don't have this kind of comfort and safety." Seth gestured at the large house. "They're more concerned about where their next meal is coming from and having a roof over their head, and if they're getting the shit beat out of them again for no reason, and a thousand other worries, *not furthering* their education. Being able to play or enjoy life without a care is a luxury they can't afford. For most of them, your rec center is the only safe place kids have for a few hours a day and escape the realities of their real lives."

Marshall studied Seth. The younger man's eyes were dulled, and his jaw tightened, but self-pity wasn't part of Seth's vocabulary.

"You're right. Let's finish our talk on the ice." Marshall opened his door.

"I guess the talking is something I can't opt out of." A smile tugged at the corners of Seth's mouth.

Seth's skating was his sole outlet for his anger, disappointment, and a way to rid himself of accumulated stress. A personal confidante wasn't a luxury for him.

CHANGED INTO THEIR HOCKEY GEAR, brand new everything for Seth, the pair spent the next two hours on the ice. Seth found it easier sharing his past with Marshall than he feared. At the conclusion of their skate, Marshall became privy to Seth's fears and dreams.

Seth stopped halfway to the house. "Can I make it, Coach?" A hint of trepidation lurked in the deep blue of his eyes.

Marshall studied the younger man. "I wouldn't be doing this if I didn't think so, but it's your decision. You have to want it, work for it. No drugs. Nothing, pot included, and no more selling yourself. That's over. Done. Finished. Focus on your game and you'll be in the big league. It won't happen overnight, but if you listen to me, and other coaches, it will happen."

"Coach, I lost my license. How will I get around?"

"Let me worry about that, you concentrate on your game."

MARSHALL LOADED the last of Seth's and his suitcases and hockey equipment into the Cayenne. The previous day, Seth, under Lauren's guidance, bought a new wardrobe. During dinner, Marshall chuckled at Lauren relaying their shopping adventures, including Seth's resistance in being fitted for several suits.

His newest prospect emerging from the house, Marshall grinned watching Seth interacting with the children. Goodbyes said, the two climbed in the SUV and embarked on the drive to Charleston, South Carolina.

Two hours into their trip, Seth said, "I can drive."

"Yeah, but you're not." Marshall smiled.

The next couple of hours passed in a mixture of silence and hockey talk. Their lunch break concluded, and the Cayenne fueled up, Marshall handed Seth a folder.

"What's this?"

"Your background."

Seth opened and read through it.

"Coach, and these?" He raised his arms.

"You were in foster care, according to the law. Keep it simple. Those..." Marshall nodded at Seth's fading track marks. "...whatever you're comfortable with."

"Okay."

"Are you okay?"

"Yeah, I'm fine." Seth forced a quick smile.

"Some friendly advice. Don't cut yourself short and not everyone is your enemy. There are good people out there."

Seth cocked his head at Marshall.

Marshall caught a flicker of sadness in Seth's eyes. "Did you come to the rink because of me?"

"Yeah."

"And you hoped I'd notice your skating, and give you this opportunity," Marshall said.

"All I wanted was to skate with my hockey idol and…maybe you'd notice me skate and say something, but I never expected or hoped for this opportunity. I just wanted something to renew my hope that maybe life was worth living." Seth leaned his head, resting it on the side window.

Marshall inhaled a breath and eased his foot off the gas pedal.

"Were you considering suicide?"

"I don't know, maybe, but I was…"

"Tempted?"

"Yeah," Seth paused, "but not anymore. Coach, I'm done with the drugs. Even the pot."

"Good. Now, let's talk hockey. We'll start a weight training, exercise, and skating regime, including a proper diet. No skipping meals. My accountant and personnel assistant will help manage your money—"

"Money? Like, how much money?"

"Does it matter?" Marshall arched a brow.

"Well, yeah. It's at least minimum wage, right?"

Marshall erupted into laughter and apologized once his mirth subsided.

"Yeah, Seth, probably a tad more. Like a lot more." Marshall smiled at Seth and explained how he negotiated a two-way contract with Boston and their American Hockey League team but assigned him to their East Coast Hockey League putting him into a higher pay bracket than the ECHL minimum.

"You're fucking joking me. What the hell do I do with that much money?" Seth braced himself against the door.

"Invest and only spend what you need. Later you can spend more, hence the accountant."

"Coach, you'll help me manage it too?"

Marshall eyed Seth, and replied, "Of course, I will. Seth, I'm here any time you need me. Whether it's a question, a concern, or a problem. Promise me, you'll always come to me if you need to talk, have a craving, anything, please come to me."

"I will. I owe you, Coach."

"No, no you don't. Play the game you love and become the best defenseman ever."

"Better than, Colin Montoya?"

"I've no doubt if you play your cards right, you'll be playing with and learning from him."

A comfortable silence stretching between them, Seth broke it.

"You saved my life, Coach."

The gratitude in the quiet assertion made Marshall pause and he glanced Seth's way.

Had he?

CHAPTER 4

The team's training camp beginning the next day, Marshall rubbed his temples and scrutinized his roster for the upcoming season. Marshall skimmed through the apartment pairings for a fourth time, and billeted Seth with forward, Logan Kennedy.

He preferred keeping same-position players together, but in this case, he needed someone with stability and a good head on their shoulders. Someone he trusted. Logan's girlfriend, Kimmie Saladyga was another good influence for his newest charge.

Marshall hated this aspect of coaching at this level. He preferred spending the time on the ice developing his players instead of shuffling papers.

The distinct thud of two pairs of skates, not three, on the carpeted floor, echoing in the hallway, brought a smile to Marshall's face. He suspected the identity of the missing skater and left his office.

Marshall stopped at the bench area and staying silent, his smile widened, and he leaned against the side of the bleachers and observed his rookie defenseman.

The previous two week's he devoted three to four hours a day working with Seth, Tyler Brennan, and their newest and unexpected acquisition fresh from Russia, Aleksander Miszczak.

Tyler's near-fatal car accident the night the Patriots won the Kelly Cup last season the sole reason, Boston assigned him here instead of starting the season there. His presence on the ice bolstered Seth's confidence, and his patience surprised Marshall.

Despite his misgivings surrounding Aleksander's arrival, Marshall appreciated his eagerness in helping Seth. To his surprise his two newest rookies formed an instant connection.

The kid exhibited more power in his skating than expected and tomorrow the true test came. Would the extra time Seth spent practicing with him, Tyler, and Aleksander pay off?

Tyler and Aleksander already in the locker room, Marshall observed Seth continuing to skate. He returned to his office and finished working on the team's apartment pairings and road trip room assignments.

Alek living in an apartment his girlfriend supplied, not to Marshall's liking, but his hands were tied on that front. He paired him with Seth for the overnight travel games.

Several loud smacks echoed around the arena, and Marshall left his office to check its source. The telltale ping of a puck hitting the cross bar on the goal net greeted him the moment he reached the ice surface.

His newest defenseman stood two feet inside the blue line, several pucks in front of him.

Each of the first two pucks Seth hit landed in separate places in the back of the net. His third sailed into the top right corner. Another hit the left side halfway between the cross bar and the ice. Four more shots followed, each reaching their target, but in various areas of the net.

His defenseman's shooting capability ranked low on Marshall's immediate priorities in developing Seth's natural skills. Instead, he focused on Seth's skating, endurance, and agility.

"Doyle." Marshall gestured for Seth.

"Hey, Coach. I hope it's okay I stayed out longer than Ty and Alek."

"Never apologize for putting in ice time. Where did you learn to shoot like that? And how the hell did you plan on getting back home?"

"Back alleys, and Uber."

"Don't move." Marshall disappeared, returning a few minutes later carrying a bucket of pucks. He joined Seth, and the two skated to the blue line and Marshall dumped the pucks. "Shoot all of them."

"Okay."

Seth fired off all ten. Two missed. He cleared the pucks from the net, sending them back to Marshall.

"Are you aiming for precise locations? Or shooting center net?"

"Location. Different goalies play the puck differently, so why shoot at the same place every time." A perplexed expression creased Seth's face.

"Shoot them where I call it. Can you do that?"

"I guess." Seth shrugged, and on Marshall's command, he struck each puck, hitting his mark.

"Fucking, shit, Doyle. Why aren't you a forward?"

"I always wanted to be one, but every coach put me on defense. I guess, because of my height. It's a good position," Seth said. The pucks gathered a third time, he added, "Am I finished?"

"Yeah, go shower." Marshall gestured at the bench and Seth skated away. "Doyle, has anyone ever clocked your shot?"

"No."

Marshall glanced at the ice, shook his head, and trailed behind his player. He finished his tasks in his office, smiling the entire time. He landed his team a big defenseman with skating skills and toughness, and a shot worthy of the best NHL forwards.

SETH EXITED Logan's Jeep and accompanied his roommate inside the arena for the team's home opener. The team having begun their season on the road, he found immediate success in his first professional game, and a needed boost to his confidence.

Inside the dressing room, Seth changed out of his jacket, slacks, and shirt. He preferred the comfort of jeans and t-shirts, but he adhered to the dress code.

The team completed their warm-up skate and gathered in the locker room.

Brad Myurzz called his name and Seth raised his eyes to the forward.

"Thackeray, number 77, is a beast. He'll take cheap shots with his stick, and he always targets the new guys."

"Yeah, he's a brute, had it in for Brennan last year. Ty smoked his ass all season." Logan smiled.

"Keep your head up, too, Alek," Brad said.

"I loved every minute of it." Tyler grinned at Seth.

"So, watch our chicklets." Seth chuckled.

"He has to catch us, right, Ty?" Aleksander's deep, accented voice reverberated around the room.

"I so want to see the bastard laid out," another of the team's defensemen, Tristian DiPaulo interjected.

Seth smiled at Tristian, then looked at Tyler and Alek. "I have your backs out there."

"Thanks." Tyler smiled and resumed dressing.

The teammates talking halted once Marshall entered the room.

"Stay focused, Doyle. Play our game, boys. Thackeray's one guy, but he can be five if we let him." Marshall paused, his gaze encompassing the room. "Ok, starting lineup. Alek, left wing. Brennan, right. Logan, center. DiPaulo, right D. Doyle, left D. Connor, you're in net. Brad, you're rotating shifts halfway through each period with Alek and Ty. Keep them off balance."

The team filing out of the locker room for the first period, Marshall grabbed Seth's wrist. The two alone, he said, "Put the fucking bastard on the ice if needed."

He grinned and hurried down the hallway and joined his teammates.

SETH's first opportunity for placing a hard, and legal hit on Thackeray occurred with five minutes left in the first period. His shoulders squared, and Thackeray concentrating on bringing the puck into the Patriots' offensive zone, he encountered a wall of six foot three, two-hundred and twenty-five-pound rookie defenseman. The impact sprawled him on his backside.

His opponent's forward progress thwarted, Seth ignored the roaring crowd and focused on the game.

Thackeray rose and skated to his bench. "Fucker's going down." Seated on the bench he located his culprit.

Seth skating past, Thackeray chirped him. "You're mine, Doyle."

Unfazed, Seth flashed Thackeray a fuck-off gesture and left the ice. Seated on the bench, he acknowledged the cheering, riled-up fans and lifted his stick in the air, inciting them into a louder frenzy.

Adam Panko, the team's assistant coach, leaned close to Seth, saying, "You'll need eyes in the back of your head for the next forty minutes."

Long ago, Seth learned a hard lesson and made the mistake of letting his guard down. He never did it again.

"Nah." Seth twisted and faced their opponent's bench and blew Thackeray a kiss.

THE PERIOD ENDED, Thackeray spied Seth, and pointed his stick. "You and me, Doyle."

Seth maintained his pace, raised his stick in acknowledgment of the threat, but brushed it off.

Inside their tunnel, Thackeray fumed, cursing and vowing vengeance.

THE BUZZER for the second period sounding, Marshall pulled Seth aside. "Watch his stick."

"Got it." Seth inclined his head. "Relax, Coach, I'm quite capable of defending myself."

"That's on the streets, Doyle. You weren't wearing hockey gear and standing on a sheet of ice."

27

"Just padding for me. I survived being jumped by six guys, years older than me, Coach. I can handle Thackeray. Just enjoy the show."

THACKERAY POSITIONED HIMSELF OPPOSITE SETH, and the testosterone-driven tension between them radiated throughout the arena.

"Fuck, not the way I want this period starting." Marshall maintained his usual placid expression, but he riveted his attention on Seth and Thackeray.

"Guess we'll see what the kid's made of, for real, now," Adam said.

"He'll win."

THE LINESMAN DROPPED the puck and Thackeray skated straight for Seth. His stick raised.

Seth pivoted, placing his back to Thackeray, and lulling his opponent into a false sense of victory. He anticipated the illegal cross check and spun around, his stick raised, he caught Thackeray's. The abrupt and unexpected move surprised his opponent and his stick clattered to the ice.

Their gloves shook off, Seth grasped the front of Thackeray's jersey, twisted, and shoved his fisted hand beneath the man's chin, throwing rapid fast punches with his other. One strike grazed the bottom of Thackeray's visor, but Seth ignored the burning pain of hard plastic scraping away layers of skin.

Seth's fourth punch cracked Thackeray's nose, spewing blood, and the man dropped to his knees. Instead of continuing the one-sided beating, Seth collected his stick and gloves and skated to the penalty box.

The crowd's screams of approval shook the arena, drowning out the thud of his teammates' sticks banging the boards. Within seconds the replay of the fight flashed across the scoreboard screens and the crowd erupted again.

Seated in the box, Seth removed his helmet, accepted the towel the box official handed him and wrapped it around his hand. A bottle of water in hand, he squirted it in his mouth, and doused his face.

"Do you need that checked?" The official gestured at Seth's hand.

"Nah, It's good."

Thackeray's teammates assisting him to his feet, he glared across the ice at Seth.

HIS FIVE-MINUTE PENALTY for fighting having expired, Seth rejoined his teammates on the ice. Seth's earlier altercation changed the course of the game and their opponent's manner of play. Florida's players skating a wide berth around Seth resulted in numerous mistakes, opening the door for several Patriots goals.

In one play, a Florida forward failing to avoid Seth in the Patriots defensive zone resulted in another turnover.

Seth extended his stick and poked the puck free from his opponent, allowing Brad to seize possession. The play enabled Brad and Tyler to utilize their speed and skate out of their defensive zone and into Florida's end of the ice.

Florida's faux pas left a sole player to confront Brad and Tyler creating the two-on-one disadvantage. Tyler notched the goal, his third, and collected a hat trick.

Seth gained another assist on the play.

The Patriots scored three additional goals and claimed the lopsided win.

UPON THE GAME'S CONCLUSION, Ansley Thomas summoned Seth to the training room once he stripped out of his uniform and equipment. Ansley, the team's assistant trainer, assumed the duties of head trainer at the onset of the season. A role normally undertaken by her uncle Neil Vokey.

Personal medical issues required Neil to take a leave of absence, but he continued assisting whenever his health permitted.

· · ·

SETH'S HAND EVALUATED, he headed for the showers.

Showered and dressed, Marshall's booming voice stopped Seth's exit from the arena, and he retraced his steps until he came face-to-face with his coach.

"Hey, Coach."

"How's the hand?" Marshall nodded at it.

"It's fine. Burns some, but it's good."

"Good, have Ansley check it each day. Go on, go." Marshall waved him away.

"Coach?"

Marshall waited, and Seth added, "I was defending myself."

"Doyle, you defended your team. I've dreamed of the day someone kicked Thackeray's ass." Marshall smiled and left.

"Thanks." Seth called after him, and hurried outside, spotting Logan and Kimmie waiting by Logan's Jeep Wrangler.

"Hi, Kimmie."

"Hey, Seth. Awesome fight. How's your hand?" She caught his fingers to study the injury mimicking a bad carpet burn.

"It's fine. Hey, I can catch a ride home with someone else or call Uber if you two want to go out."

"We're meeting the other guys for wings. Come with us. It'll be fun," Logan said.

"Sure."

The three piled into the Jeep.

WITHIN MINUTES of the players occupying several tables near the bar, a brunette sidled alongside Seth. Her endowed cleavage extended the limits of her low-cut shirt and she pressed herself against his arm. She trolled her manicured fingers along his thigh.

The woman's roving hand left Seth unfazed.

Her mouth near his ear she spoke into it. "Great game, Seth. You sure planted Thackeray on his ass. I'm a nurse and happy to attend to your hand."

Seth cocked his head in her direction, his eyes taking in her show of cleavage. "What if my hand isn't what needs attending?"

He winked at his friends.

"My mouth is always moist." The woman pressed closer to Seth and nuzzled the side of his neck.

"For the love of God, I'm going to barf." Kimmie, seated across from Seth, rolled her eyes and sipped her drink.

"Go for it." Brad waved his hand, urging his friend to accept the woman's offer.

"Bradley." Victoria Vavasseur smacked her boyfriend's arm.

"What? She offered giving him a blow job." Brad shrugged and threw his hands in the air. A wide smile slid across his face, and he dodged Victoria's punch.

"Ugh, you're all the same." Victoria shook her head and glared at Brad.

Seth playing off his friends' encouragement, wrapped his arm around the woman's waist, pulled her into him, and she swung her leg, straddling his lap.

A barrage of catcalls from his teammates and the woman said, "Let's go somewhere private."

"This is becoming a live porn movie." Logan chimed in and suffered Kimmie's elbow jabbing his ribs.

"Only if you come to my place, but after we eat. Pull up a chair…" Seth surveyed the curvy brunette. *What the hell. Why not?*

"My name is Sonia, and I'll come wherever, handsome." She grabbed a chair from another table and placed it next to Seth's.

Kimmie and Victoria exchanged eye rolls, and each cast glares of disapproval at the newcomer.

Their meal finished, Seth rose, and his hand on Sonia's back, escorted her away from the table.

Additional catcalls from his teammates followed them out of the restaurant.

SETH WAKING in the morning with a bed partner, a normal occurrence for him, woke Sonia and ushered her out of the apartment. Dressed in workout attire, he left the apartment and entered the complex's exercise room. He completed his three-mile ride on the stationary bike and pumped some iron.

Upon his return to the apartment, he showered, fixed an ice bag for his hand, and joined Kimmie and Logan in the living room.

"I can't believe you brought her home." Kimmie eyed Seth, but a smile crept to her face.

"I shouldn't have, and I'm sorry, Kimmie."

"Didn't bother me," Logan said.

"It's fine. You two better go. You don't want to be late for practice." Kimmie rose and headed to her bedroom.

"You didn't have to leave. No kiss?" Logan shouted.

"I'm taking a shower."

Seth nodded in the direction of the bedrooms. "You have time." His laughter chasing Logan darting out of the living room and hightailing it after his girlfriend.

CHAPTER 5

Seth suppressed a yawn and collected his equipment bag and suitcase from the bus's cargo area. He heaved the bag onto his shoulder and wheeled the suitcase across the arena's parking lot.

His gear hung in his equipment stall, he gripped his suitcase and made for the locker room door. "Logan, I'll meet you outside."

"Be there in five."

Halfway down the hallway Marshall's voice summoned him. Seth yawned, turned, and wove around team personnel. He propped his wary body against the doorframe of Marshall's office and worked the kinks out of his neck.

"Have your shoulder evaluated tomorrow. We'll see whether you're in a non-contact jersey or off the ice. Oh, and these came." Marshall handed Seth an envelope.

"Can I weight train?" Seth asked, eyeing the envelope.

"Let's see what tomorrow's assessment reveals. We need you for the long run. Open it." Marshall nodded at the envelope.

Seth ripped open the envelope and removed the items within. "So, I can drive now?"

"Yup."

"Uh...I...uh could...uh, buy a car?"

"You don't need to buy a car, Seth."

"Oh, okay. I better go, Logan's waiting." Seth levered himself off the doorframe.

"Seth, wait."

Marshall rose from his chair and rounded the desk. He closed his office door and ushered Seth forward. Outside the arena Seth surveyed the area for his roommate's Jeep or Kimmie's car.

"Uh, Coach, I uh, need a ride. I guess Logan was tired of waiting."

"I'm the one needing the ride. Here." Marshall dropped the key fob for his Cayenne in Seth's hand.

Seth stared at the keys for the expensive vehicle.

"Let's go. I'll explain on the way."

SETH PARKED the Porsche outside his apartment and lingered inside the expensive luxury vehicle. Dramatic changes occurred in his life the past three months, for the better, and he smiled. He exited the vehicle and paused. The hairs on his nape prickled.

He squinted into the dimness of the parking lot. Years of homelessness honed his survival instincts, and his gut and intuition ensured his survival. A near-death experience during his first year of homeless living taught Seth to heed the warning of a lurking unwanted presence.

His gaze traveled between the various buildings. Movement and voices coming from one of the balconies snagged his interest. One of his teammates waved, and Seth reciprocated the greeting and headed for his residence.

Seth paused at his door. His suitcase deposited, he strolled to the end of the corridor overlooking the parking lot. He squinted, scanning the deeper shadows near the buildings and between the parked cars. A shadowy figure hurried between two mid-sized SUVs, and scurried along the building opposite his, and disappeared.

Once inside his apartment, Seth closed the blinds for the sliding glass door leading to the balcony and did the same in his bedroom. Both faced the parking lot.

Changed into a pair of sleep shorts, he sank onto his bed, but despite his physical and mental fatigue, sleep eluded him.

Seth locked his hands behind his head and stared at the rotating fan blades. They spun around and around in a continuous circle mimicking his merry-go-round life in foster care. His sixth sense solidified his suspicion. The slinking figure he spied earlier wasn't a complex resident. His familiar gait shot chills along Seth's spine.

His probation officer the only person he knew of with knowledge of his whereabouts…or was he? The question haunted Seth long past the sun rising for a new day. Accustomed to minimal hours of sleep, he rose, completed his usual morning routine, and drove to the team doctor's office for his appointment.

Seth stayed on high alert from the time he left until he reached the arena. Parked in the designated player parking, he scanned his surroundings. Assured of his safety, he exited the SUV, and locked it.

NATALIE SAVAGE ENTERED the hockey arena and hugged her best friend, Moira Benton. The two meandered through the arena, swapping work stories until the pair arrived at the Mills' suite. Moira's boyfriend, Cooper Mills, the Patriots' general manager shared owner-ship of the team with his twin sister Ashley, their father, and grandmother.

"Glad you made it tonight," Cooper said. He greeted Moira with a kiss and hugged Natalie.

"Finally, I have a game day off. I can make it tomorrow too. Yay." Natalie accepted the opened beer Moira handed her. "And enjoy a few of these. My bestie here is driving." She slapped Moira on the arm.

"Tying one on tonight?" Moira giggled and sipped her drink.

"No."

"Ladies, I've some team matters to take care of before puck drop." Cooper left the suite.

"Coop, is Doyle in the lineup?" Moira asked and directed her next words to Natalie. "He's been scratched from the lineup the past few games because of an injury."

"I believe so." He smiled and left.

"Great! Nat, wait until you see Seth Doyle. Six-three, two-hundred plus pounds of muscle and damn he can skate, and he'll hit. Awesome fighter too."

"What color eyes?"

"Blue. Deep blue. He's number twenty-two, a defenseman." Moira finished off her beer and sank into a chair.

Natalie dropped into a seat alongside Moira's and opened the team's program book. She flipped through it, finding the roster, twisted, and faced her friend.

"Moira, he's twenty-one!"

"So, it's easier training him. Cooper's younger than me." Moira shrugged her shoulders.

"By what? A year? Not eight!" The players skating onto the ice for warm-ups brought Natalie to the edge of her seat.

"Hey, ninety percent of these guys are young pups. It's your choice, girlfriend." Moira kicked her feet out in front of her and relaxed.

"Hi, Moira," Kimmie and Victoria said entering the suite.

"Hey, Kimmie, Victoria, this is my best friend, Natalie. We work together. Nat's a K-9 officer. I'm hoping to set her up with Seth."

"Oh, you'll like him. He's super nice and a hottie too, but don't tell Logan." Kimmie laughed and fanned her face.

"Seth rooms with Logan Kennedy, Kimmie's boyfriend," Moira explained.

"Then, I'll check this guy out." Natalie leaned forward, her hands clasped together, wrists on the top of the wall separating the suite's seats from the regular ones.

"There, twenty-two," Victoria pointed at Seth.

"Isn't that ironic, one number above his age." Natalie rolled her eyes.

"Come on, Nat, look at his positioning," Moira said, cocking her head in Seth's direction.

Natalie, along with Kimmie and Victoria turned their attention to

Seth on his knees slowly spreading them apart until his muscles reach their limit. Him leaning forward, his hands on the ice, mimicking a slight thrusting motion, working his hips forward and backward, loosening up, brought a low gasp from Natalie.

The seductiveness of the simple stretch knocked all four women's minds onto the path of sexual thoughts, and watched in awe, cocking their heads in unison.

Moira broke the spell, saying, "Just imagine yourself naked beneath him." Her shoulder bumping Natalie's, she added, "Damn, that stretch is sexy."

"Yeah, it is." Natalie replied but her eyes stayed fixed on Seth.

Kimmie and Victoria erupted into laughter and their banter persisted throughout the warm-ups.

Natalie eyed Seth Doyle during the pre-game skate. His helmet's visor and the distance between the ice and suite distorted her view of his facial features. She preferred a nice-on-the-eyes guy. He appeared well built but his equipment made it impossible to tell.

The team exiting the ice, Moira pinned Natalie with an unrelenting gaze. "So."

"Looks cute but can't say for sure."

"Hey, Kimmie, you have any pictures of Seth on your phone?" Moira swung around.

"Uh, let me look. Nope, sorry."

"If he's starting, they'll show his face on the scoreboard during the starting lineup intro," Victoria said.

"I'll bet there's another fight between him and Thackeray. He'll be out for revenge," Kimmie said.

"No doubt." Moira rose and fixed a plate of snacks. She convinced Cooper the box needed a better array of refreshments, and he obliged.

"Why was he out? From the previous fight?" Natalie joined Moira at the counter and filled a plate.

"Oh, no. Thackeray never landed a punch. Seth beat the shit out of him. He injured his shoulder a few games ago," Victoria supplied.

The four friends chatted and snacked until the buzzer sounded for the start of the game. This time Natalie, along with Moira, Victoria, and Kimmie stood at the suite's edge for the player introductions.

Seth's face flashed on the jumbotron upon his introduction as one of the starting defensemen, Natalie's three friends spoke in unison. "Well?"

"Yeah, he's hot, but he's just a pup." Natalie smiled.

"Forget the damn age difference, Nat. A guy with his muscles will put the puck in the net." Moira grinned and eyed her friend.

"Hmm, is there something Cooper needs to know?" Natalie's smile widened and the friends erupted into laughter.

"Dare I ask what I'm supposed to know." Cooper's voice boomed behind them.

"Hey, Coop. Nothing." Moira snuggled into his arms and kissed him.

"She told Nat to trust her, and that Seth Doyle could put the puck in her net," Victoria said.

Natalie choked on her laughter and Kimmie joined her.

"Uh, thanks. TMI ladies. Let's watch the game." Cooper shook his head, made a plate of food, and seated himself alongside Moira.

Natalie chose a seat on the other side of her best friend.

Kimmie and Victoria selected seats at the end of the row.

"Will Thackeray target Seth?" Moira addressed her question to Cooper.

"I'd say there's a good chance he will. Marshall will avoid having them on the ice together, but not at the expense of the team winning."

SETH HEADED out of the locker room, but Marshall halted his progress.

"I know, Coach. Keep my head on a swivel."

"Do what's necessary, but do *not* initiate it." Marshall patted Seth's forearm and ushered him toward the tunnel.

His name called for the introductions, Seth skated to their defensive blue line, his eyes colliding with Thackeray's.

The man's stayed riveted on him.

Seth avoided any direct contact with Thackeray on his first three shifts. On the fourth one, the play provided Thackeray his opportunity for payback, and he seized it.

His shoulder bracing himself against the boards, Seth battled for possession of the puck. He kicked it free and spun around.

Thackeray plowed into him and driving Seth into the glass. His stick held in both hands, he shoved it in Seth's face and the two tumbled to the ice. Thackeray on top of Seth.

Stars danced across Seth's vision from the impact of the stick striking his face and his head slamming into the plexiglass. His street survival instincts kicked in and he tipped his head, avoiding a punch in the nose. The blow hammered his cheek. Seth grunted, gritted his teeth, and shoved Thackeray off him.

Seth ignored the gash on his cheekbone and the bridge of his nose. On his way to his feet, he grabbed Thackeray's jersey, yanking his nemesis up off the ice and leveled a punishing right uppercut beneath Thackeray's chin.

The blow stunned his opponent and dropped him back to the ice.

Seth ignored the blood streaming down his cheek and skated toward his bench.

"Fucking shit." Marshall clenched his fist and cut a look at Seth stepping off the ice and heading into the tunnel with Ansley.

SETH EASED onto the exam table in the training room and held the towel Ansley handed him upon his exit from the ice, staunching the blood flow. His cheek throbbed and his eye burned.

He lowered the towel and water spilled from his eye and Ansley examined the injury.

"We'll have the ophthalmologist check you. How is your vision?"

"A little blurry. Stings like a mother fucker, sorry, and it won't stop watering." Seth grimaced with the effort of holding his eye open while Ansley flashed a pen light at it.

"Pupils are reactive, that's a good sign. I suspect a corneal abrasion. Nose isn't broken, but I can't rule out a fractured cheekbone or sinus cavity. Here." Ansley handed him a clean towel.

Seth arched an eyebrow.

"Blow your nose."

His cheek not puffing out when he blew into the towel, she said, "Good. We'll do X-rays to make sure there are no fractures. How is the shoulder? That was a hard hit."

"Sore, but it's good." Seth slid off the table and stripped off his jersey and shoulder pads.

"Have a seat." Ansley cleaned away the blood, inspected his facial wounds, followed by a quick assessment of his shoulder, and conducted her portion of the required concussion protocol tests.

"Do I have to go to the hospital?"

"Not for the X-rays but league concussion protocol requires you to go. Let's get those images done. The tech won't want to hang around any longer than necessary. He's not a big hockey fan," Ansley replied and gestured at the door.

"We do them here?" Seth followed Ansley.

"Yup. State-of-the-art stuff here. This arena is a dream to work and play in at this level. It rivals some of the best NHL ones. The Mills family takes care of their team."

"I'd say so."

"We'll have your shoulder checked at the hospital too. Do you have a headache? Any dizziness?" Ansley eyed him during their walk to the room housing the portable X-ray machine. She scrutinized his features, searching for any indication he lied. Hockey players weren't forthcoming with injuries, including possible concussions.

"No, considering the asshole slammed my head into the boards and his stick in my face." Seth entered the X-ray room. The technician grunted his reply greeting and directed him for the needed images.

A team assistant waiting outside the room, Ansley left and arranged for his departure.

Upon Seth's return to the training room, Marshall entered and opened his mouth to speak.

"I'm fine, Coach. I'm sure it looks worse than it is. Ansley's sending me to the hospital." Seth removed the ice pack revealing the bruising, discoloration, and cuts. One beneath his right eye, the other on the bridge of his nose.

"How is the vision?" Marshall studied his young defenseman.

"Better, until my eye starts watering." Seth replaced the ice pack.

"How are you feeling?"

"Coach, I'm fine."

"Look, Seth, concussions are nothing to mess with," Marshall said and observed his player's movements, overall speech, and pronunciation.

"I'm fine, really. Okay, my face hurts like hell. I'm sure yours would too, if some asshole smashed a hockey stick into it and shoved your face into the boards." Seth met Marshall's eyes.

"Yeah, it would, and it has. I'll come to the hospital once the game is finished. I'll have Lauren go with you."

"Thanks, but a hospital isn't a place for kids to be hanging out in. I'm good, Coach."

"You're sure?"

"Thanks, Coach. I appreciate it, but I got this."

"You're welcome. I'll be by after the game to pick you up."

CHAPTER 6

Tremaine Kingston lounged on his couch, beer in one hand, cigarette in the other, and two girls in his lap. One of his cronies entering the room prompted him shoving aside the female kissing him.

"He's in South Carolina and driving a Porsche." The man accepted a beer, sipped it, and sank into a chair. Another female positioned herself on his lap.

"Interesting." Tremaine inhaled a long drag on his cigarette.

"Tre, he ain't saying nothing. Forget him. He's more trouble than he's worth."

"You know the rules. *No* one leaves me, and he's costing me a lot of money. His regulars are complaining. I should've kept him as my personal cock-sucking pleasure bitch." Tremaine chugged his beer and demanded another.

"You gonna kill him?"

"Maybe, or hook his ass again, then kill him."

"You want Ice to stay down there?"

Tremaine nodded.

NATALIE FLEXED her neck several times, easing the stiffness from sitting in the patrol unit observing the suspected drug house. Three hours into the stakeout involving a high-level Chicago drug trafficking gang member, and nothing.

She wriggled in her seat, peering through the cage separating the vehicle's front and rear seats, and addressed Elvis, her K-9 partner. The dog's composed behavior confirmed her suspicions. Ice, the perp, no longer occupied the area. Early in their working relationship, Elvis exhibited several unique behaviors, and she trusted his instincts.

ELVIS' odd behavior first manifested during a raid on a suspected meth house. A search of the home yielded nothing, not one shred of evidence of drugs being manufactured there, despite Elvis and two other canine's alerting.

Natalie, positioned near the doorway of the last room to search, a laundry in the rear of the home. Prior to them entering and clearing it, Elvis' frantic barking preceded all hell breaking loose. The dog jerked on his leash with such force, he yanked Natalie to the floor seconds prior to an explosion. Splintered wood, a scorching wave of heat and flame engulfed the doorway and surrounding area.

Elvis tugging on his leash, dragged an unconscious Natalie away from the burning room.

NATALIE SHOOK ASIDE her memory and focused out the window. Another two hours passed, and the team called it a night.

Her cruiser parked, she exited the vehicle, and opened the rear door. Elvis bounded out and stretched. "Sorry, boy. I enjoyed it as much as you did. Come on." She grabbed the dog's lead, and the pair entered their residence.

Natalie placed Elvis' food bowl on the floor and leaned against the counter. "So, do I bother with this guy? He's eight years younger than me, but damn, Elvis, he's hot."

The dog paused eating, his head tilting to the side.

"I guess that's a yes."

Elvis resumed eating his meal and Natalie disappeared in her bedroom. Changed out of her uniform, she flopped onto the bed, and Elvis joined her.

She suppressed a yawn and texted Moira. Without waiting for a reply, she slid beneath the covers, and slept.

NATALIE'S PHONE ringing woke her from a dead sleep, and grunting, she rolled toward the irritating noise. She fumbled around on the nightstand, located her phone, and noted the caller's name, Moira.

"Hey." Natalie listened to her best friend and bolted into a sitting position. "Like, in right now?"

She checked the time on her phone and swore. The call disconnected, she swung her legs off the bed, and hurried into the bathroom, washed, and dressed in record time. No time for applying makeup, she pinched her cheeks, and did a brief facial inspection.

"Come on boy, let's go out. Auntie Moira will be here any minute."

Back in the apartment, Natalie squatted in front of Elvis' crate. "Wish me luck, boy."

Elvis' single bark halted her.

"Yeah, yeah, you can approve. I promise. Later." Natalie hurried out and met Moira halfway between the parking lot and her apartment.

"Long night?"

"Yeah, and nothing. Waste of a night off."

"Going for the natural look, I see."

"Uh, it was either stink or do my makeup. Besides he'll either like me or not." Natalie climbed into the passenger seat of Moira's SUV.

"True, besides what does it matter what you look like when you're getting laid." Moira chuckled and put the vehicle in gear.

"You're bad. He might not be interested," Natalie said.

"True, but rumor has it, he's easy." Moira winked.

"Great. Now you tell me he's a playboy."

"You've been so hung up on his age, I figured it didn't matter. It's not like you're marrying him."

"It concerns me, but he's trainable, right?"

The two laughed and chatted during the drive to the hockey arena.

SETH LACKED people skills and refrained from interacting unless required. Today's event required his participation. His ingrained suspicion others were using him for their personal gain waned each day. Seth's past prevented extending his trust to anyone other than Marshall.

His skates laced, he shrugged into his jersey, and left the locker room.

"Hey, Seth, wait up." Logan called out, and Seth waited in the hallway.

Logan caught up and pressed a black sharpie into his hand. "Autographs," he explained, answering Seth's unspoken question.

"I doubt I'll need it."

"You'll need it, trust me. Want to bet how many phone numbers your given?" Logan chuckled and extended his hand.

"What?"

"It'll be mostly kids, the season ticket holders and booster club people but there'll be bunnies too. They go for the new guys. Last year they chased Tyler, but he's dating Ashley Mills, and Natasha, the Russian Ice Queen, won't let them near Alek. She's one badass chick," Logan said and the two entered the tunnel leading to the ice.

"Great. So, how long does this skate last?"

"Two hours max. Hey, Moira. Where's Cooper?"

"Hi, Logan. Hi, Seth. He's coming. Is Kimmie here?"

"Not yet, but she will be. I'll see you on the ice, Seth." Logan slapped Seth's arm and left. The way Moira's friend eyed Seth wasn't lost on him, and her discreet nod his cue to leave.

Seth greeted Moira and exchanged a smile with her friend, a brunette, and followed Logan.

"Seth, wait. Natalie's still learning. I'd appreciate it if you stayed close to her."

"Uh, sure." Seth's eyes darted between Moira and her friend.

"Great. Oh…right…sorry. Natalie. Seth. Seth. Natalie." Moira wasted no time rushing away and leaving them alone.

"Hi." Natalie extended her hand.

"Hi." Seth's smile brightened once their hands clasped together.

"I'm sorry Moira put you on the spot. I'll be fine out there. I have these." Natalie tapped her knee pads and elbow pads. She patted her butt, adding, "And I have plenty of padding here."

Seth angled his body and peered behind her. "Just the right amount." His eyes riveted on the light brown of hers.

"Wow, you're straightforward. Not sure if I'm insulted or flattered." Natalie scrutinized Seth. The team program listed him at six-three, his skates adding inches, she flexed her neck from craning it upward.

"Sorry."

"For offering your opinion?"

Words eluded Seth. He kept any social interaction with the opposite sex to a bare minimum unless he…he pushed those images from his mind.

"You, okay?" Natalie's hand gripped Seth's arm. Heat pooled beneath her palm and electrified her blood. A pleasurable ache rocketed into her core.

"Uh, yeah. I better go." Seth mustered a faint smile. He paused a few steps away from her, his smile widening. "Are you coming?"

"Yeah." Natalie raked her gaze along his body. His jeans emphasized the powerful muscles beneath, and longing swept her.

SETH STEPPED out on the ice and skated with ease. He circled around, coming to an abrupt stop in front of Natalie, showering her legs with snow.

"Thanks for the ice bath." Natalie shook each foot.

"Sorry." Seth grinned and held out his hand. "I won't let you fall, promise."

"Damn, because I'd hoped you'd land on top of me if I did."

A woman flirting with him wasn't a new experience. His inner voice warned him to avoid making a big deal out of it. The bunnies flirted all the time.

"I'm kidding," Natalie said, but she lied. She wanted his awesome physique covering her, loving her. Her acute powers of observation, a necessary skill for her occupation, but Seth Doyle perplexed her.

A dark mystery surrounded him despite his polite mannerism and smoking-hot physique, and her gut warned he hid something sinister and unusual for a pro hockey player. The team's roster details provided basic information. Natalie wanted more than his age, height, weight, birthplace, and the position he played.

"That's too bad. I'd have obliged." He grinned and clutched her hand. A fiery spark twinkled in his blue eyes.

"I'm sure. Now, no laughing." Natalie's hand in his, the contact scorched her flesh, and a raging inferno consumed her despite the chill coming off the ice.

Natalie planted one foot on the ice and lifting the other over the lip in the boards she stumbled. "Aw, shit. This is embarrassing."

Seth's free arm snaked around her and prevented her fall. Their gazes connected and the two stared at each other. A half minute later, Seth pushed them away from the boards.

"Uh, Seth there's nothing to hold on to out here. Can we stay near the boards, please." Natalie tightened her grip on his hand, her nails digging in.

"Trust me."

He skated them one circuit around the ice, and started a second, but a group of boys clad in their hockey jerseys stopped them.

"Seth, can we have your autograph?"

"You're awesome. We love when you fight," another said.

"Yeah. You let 'em have it." A third chimed in, handing Seth a puck.

"Your girlfriend isn't too steady on her feet, is she?" The fourth youngster eyed Natalie and waggled his eyebrows at her.

The slew of questions brought a chuckle from Seth. Natalie did her best staying upright, one hand clutching his jersey, using it for a safety line.

"Cut her a break guys, she's learning. And fighting isn't a good thing. Don't fight unless you're provoked, and then, avoid it if possible."

"She's pretty, so it makes up for not being able to skate." The youngest of the boys shot Natalie a smile of admiration.

"Thanks, I appreciate the vote of confidence." Natalie fake frowned.

"I'll keep her." Seth winked and repositioned his weight, making it easier reaching the items the youngsters handed him.

Natalie's legs buckled.

Seth pulled her tight against him, keeping her from falling, and he met her eyes. Her light brown depths mesmerized him

"Seth, the boys." Natalie nodded at his fans.

"Yeah. Here, hold tight." Seth maneuvered her behind him, and her arms circled his waist.

A jolt of desire clutched his groin. He viewed sex in a different manner than most men. In the past it was a way of life, and one he preferred forgetting. He pleasured his partner and expected nothing in return, nor did he receive it.

Sex kept food in his mouth, provided semi-safe places to sleep, and a way to obtain the drugs he craved. Now he engaged in sex out of habit and having nothing better to occupy his spare time.

Natalie ignited new and foreign emotions, eliciting a whole new craving. To experience intimacy, not just sex. He suspected she recip-rocated his sexual interest but questioned if she was one of the groupies Logan mentioned. She was Moira's friend making him doubt her bunny status.

"Thanks, Seth." Each boy conveyed their thanks with an added good luck. One boy encouraged his idol to kick someone's ass in their next game, and Seth issued an immediate reprimand.

"You're a natural," Natalie said, and grasped the rock-solid muscles of his torso. Her death grip slackened on his jersey, and she eased around from behind him.

Images of her hands on his bare flesh flooded her mind, and lust pulsed through her body. Natalie wanted Seth more than she'd ever wanted anyone.

"Thanks. Not really."

Seth intertwined their fingers, and he skated them around the ice, completing three laps. He stopped several times for pictures and autographs.

"Hey, guys." Moira and Cooper joined the couple loitering near one of the goal nets.

The four chatted for a few minutes and Natalie excused herself. Obligations to stay on the ice and skate with the fans, Seth guided her to the bench area.

He agreed to join the trio for an early dinner after the event.

Moira joined Natalie, gulped down a bottle of water, and spoke, "So?"

"He's super-hot. Oh, my God, I'd jump him in a minute." Natalie waggled her brows at Moira.

"He's hot as hell without a shirt and in compression shorts. Don't tell Cooper I drooled over another guy, please." Moira shoulder bumped her friend.

"You're cruel."

"I've an idea." Moira outlined her plan and the two giggled and plotted.

CHAPTER 7

M oira insisted on a booth, and the couples settled in. The foursome ordered their drinks and appetizers and fell into a relaxed conversation.

Cooper, aware of Seth's background, directed their chatter to hockey and the general Charleston area.

Their meals eaten, Cooper paid the bill, and the foursome left the restaurant. The group having ridden together in Moira's SUV, they returned to the arena for Seth and Cooper to collect their cars.

Moira's suggestion kept both men from exiting the vehicle. "Now is a good time to help Natalie improve her skating. Coop has keys for the arena."

"I'm sure Seth has better things to do this evening," Natalie said, crossing her fingers in her lap.

"It's okay with me," Cooper said without missing a beat. Moira having already shared her plan to make sure Natalie and Seth had time alone.

"I'm game." Seth's gaze met Natalie's.

"Uh, okay, remember, I rode with you.." Her focus swung Moira's way.

"I'll ride with Coop and leave—"

"I can drive her."

Natalie stayed silent. Her desire for Seth igniting wicked images in her mind. *Yeah, you can drive me all right. Hard and fast and all night.*

A soft smile lighting her face, she shrugged and agreed.

Cooper unlocked the arena and deactivating the alarm, he showed Seth where the lights for the ice were. He flipped a few switches and handed Seth the keys. "Make sure to lock up and reset the alarm."

THE COUPLE'S FIRST DESTINATION, the equipment room. Seth and Natalie stopped next in the locker room and swapped out their shoes for skates.

Seth crouched in front of her, lacing her skates, she resisted sliding off the bench, bringing them level and kissing him. Instead, she said, "Seth, I don't want you feeling roped into this."

His head rising, she lifted her gaze and met his blue eyes and Natalie's heart thudded in her chest.

"If I did, I'd have said no."

"Good. Can I be honest? I can tell you're the up-front, tell-it-as-it-is type."

"Yeah, I am." He rose to his feet.

"Moira, Cooper, and I did conspire, but I—"

"Am I complaining?"

"No." Natalie studied him for a full sixty seconds. A devilish twinkle in her eyes, she grinned, and added, "We can skip the skating lesson."

"Nope. More reason for me to warm you later." Seth clutched her hand and tugged her closer, pinning her against him.

"Promise, Mr. Doyle?" Natalie ran her hands from his butt to his shoulders.

Seth's words warmed her lips. "I never break a promise."

Instead of kissing her, he eased away, and led her through the tunnel.

· · ·

SETH GUIDED Natalie around the rink, her skating becoming more fluid, and she stumbled less. She glanced at him several times, unable to hold back her smiles of triumph.

"You're doing great."

"Can I try on my own?" Comfortable with only the two of them on the ice, Natalie's bravery increased.

"Okay. I'll give you a push. Ready?" Seth positioned his hands on her waist.

"Ready." Natalie's enthusiasm rang in the single word.

Seth nudged her forward and off she went. Her confidence growing, she picked up speed, and he trailed behind.

"Shit, Seth, I can't stop. Help." Her shriek brought him power skating in her direction.

"Use the boards."

"What?" Natalie turned and lost her balance.

Seth charged toward her, and catching her at the boards, his momentum propelled them into the barrier. Seth's muscular body sandwiched Natalie between himself and the boards and plexiglass.

His chest heaving from the hard skate, he asked. "You, okay?"

Natalie swallowed hard, her answer low and breathless. "Yeah. Seth?"

Seth lifted her hair and kissed the side of her neck. Her head tipped away from him, exposing more skin and Seth seared a path along her sensitive flesh until he reached her ear lobe. His teeth nipped the tender lobe.

He tugged her shirt free of her pants. His fingers skimmed across her abdomen, and beneath the lacy material of her bra. Seth cupped her breast and teased a nipple into a hardened peak.

His other hand dipped inside the front of Natalie's pants and slipping beneath her underwear, he palmed her heated core.

Natalie moaned and ground her butt against the hard bulge straining against his jeans.

Seth's breath scorched her neck, and he slipped one finger inside her. "This?"

"God, yes." Natalie shuffled her feet outward, allowing him better access but he pushed them together.

His fingers wrought havoc on her core and nub. Natalie writhed, desperate for the release of her oncoming orgasm, but Seth held her tight, his body wedged her in place, increasing pressure on her pleasure points.

He sought the spots guaranteed to elicit guttural moans and explored until he discovered what she liked best.

Natalie's body responding, Seth nipped at her neck murmuring. "Here?"

"Yes."

"Better?"

"Oh, oh."

Seth relaxed the pressure of his finger, prompting her to beg.

"Tell me what you want." Seth's heated breath ignited a fire along her neck, and he sucked on the side of her throat awaiting her reply.

"Don't stop. Oh, God that—"

"Let go. Come for me."

"Yes, but it feels…Oh there."

"Here?" Again, Seth eased his finger away.

"No, Seth, please, you know where. God please." Natalie's voice raised and she sucked in a lung full of air.

"You're not ready."

"For God's sake yes…oh…" A series of drawn out 'Oh's' erupted, and Natalie begged Seth for release.

"Now, Seth, now!"

Seth pumped his finger, whipping her into a frenzy and rocketing her ecstasy skyward to incredible heights.

"I'm going to die." Her cheek pressing against the glass, her breath fogged the surface.

"No, you're coming so fucking hard it's making me want to come." Seth slowed his strokes.

Natalie screamed his name, and her climax burst upon her. The arena darkened, her head spun, and every nerve fiber of her being, hummed. Her core throbbed with pleasure.

The instant Natalie's orgasm subsided, Seth resumed his onslaught, spiraling her into a second more intense one. Her feet slid from under her, but Seth's body braced hers, eliminating her from falling.

He scooped her into his arms and skated off the ice.

NATALIE'S ATTENTION never wavered from Seth during the drive from the arena to her apartment. Her mind battled making the first move or wait on him.

Despite their mind-blowing intimacy at the rink, something about it tugged at her mind. His mesmerizing gaze, muscular physique, and drop-dead-gorgeous looks overshadowed the age difference concern.

Seth Doyle's earlier sexual proficiency suggestive of an older, more experienced, and mature man. Natalie wasn't complaining, but it sparked her curiosity.

Once Seth parked the Cayenne, she faced him, her gaze raking him, and her breath hitched.

He spoke first.

"Are you inviting me in?"

The seductive undertone dripping off his question stole Natalie's words, and she nodded her head. Seth opening her door, snapped her out of her fixation, and she lowered her feet to the pavement. Seth's solid presence blocked her.

Natalie stepped closer, slid her hands up his arms, and she entwined her fingers around his nape. Her lips poised to capture his, he jerked his mouth away and kissed her throat. His aversion to kissing stunned Natalie.

Seth's avoidance of the intimacy of kissing on the mouth reactionary. Instead, he scattered kisses along Natalie's throat, licking, and sucking on her tender flesh.

Natalie tucked a finger beneath his chin and forced his gaze to hers.

Seth stepped backward and grasped Natalie's hand and leading her away from the car further perplexing her.

On their walk to her apartment, her questions whirled in her mind and at the top of the list, why was he avoiding kissing on the mouth.

The two reaching her apartment threshold, she found her voice.

"I have a dog, but he's in a kennel."

"Dogs are cool."

"He's a working dog, Seth. A narcotic dog." Natalie noted the change in his posture.

"Okay." Seth doubted the dog hitting on him. The last time he mainlined hard drugs was eighteen months ago. He enjoyed the occasional joint afterward but stopped smoking a few weeks prior to meeting Marshall.

"You, okay? Something I should know?" Natalie propped herself against the doorframe.

"Nope." He opened the door and stepped aside, allowing Natalie to enter first.

Inside the apartment, Natalie gestured at the sofa and Seth seated himself and she attended to Elvis. The dog back in his kennel, she returned to the living room.

She admired Seth's body, studying it on her stroll toward him. The open V of his button-front shirt beckoned her to explore what lay beneath the fabric.

Natalie stopping in front of him, straddled his leg, and her gaze locked on his.

His hands raising, palms up, she clasped them. Her knees on either side of his waist, Natalie's mouth descended to his. Again, he evaded the kiss, his lips seeking her throat.

Natalie straightened and crossed her arms. "Why won't you kiss me?"

Seth studied Natalie, his brain in turmoil. During his days turning tricks, kissing on the mouth was off-limits. The act too personal and the one area of sex he lacked finesse in, and he feared her judgement.

His expertise lay in eliciting a woman's pleasure without any emotion or enjoyment for himself. With Natalie, he yearned letting the passion in, reaching the peak of ecstasy together, sharing the euphoria of making love, instead of going through the mechanical motions of having sex because it was expected.

Undeterred, Natalie used her authoritative tone. "Kiss me, Seth. On the mouth."

A third pass, and he relented. Her lips brushed his. The kiss soft and tender, but exploratory.

The contact kindled an exciting sensation deep inside Seth. He released her hand and cupped her head. Her lips parting, her tongue tasting his lips, he opened his mouth.

Her tongue grazed his and Seth moaned. A spark ignited and a blaze raced through him, and her body molded to his. Their tongues clashed in a wild dance for dominance.

Natalie unbuttoned and tugged at Seth's shirt and discarded it.

Her top and bra followed.

Natalie murmured beneath his lower lip. "Now, Seth."

Stripped out of their clothing, his rock-hard, masculine body pressed hers into the couch, and pitched her world into a tailspin.

Habit prompted Seth's question. "Quick or drawn out?"

"I don't care." His question perplexing, but desire overrode her need for clarification.

Natalie reached between her legs, circling his swollen member, and gasped. His size concerned her but the thick flesh in her hand heightened her anticipation of a wild ride into sexual bliss.

Natalie thrummed with need during the time needed for him to roll on a condom.

Seth raised her ankles onto his shoulders and sank into her. He paused for the briefest time. Her body adjusted to him, and he set a punishing rhythm.

Her sheath, hot and tight around him, he reveled in the sensations roaring through him. For the first time in his life, Seth hungered for the sexual bliss denied him in prior sexual encounters.

"Natalie." Her name dragged out on a guttural moan.

"Seth, love me." Natalie bucked her hips into his.

Seth obliged and he pumped hard and furious into her. Natalie's nails dug into his waist, leaving deep bruises, and scratching his skin.

Sucked into a dizzying vortex, the crescendo hovered, and together they crashed over the cliff into ecstasy.

SETH'S RELEASE INTOXICATING. The world around him disappeared, and he slumped against Natalie.

Natalie, trembling from her orgasm, undulated under Seth, wanting more.

THEIR BREATHING SLOWING, sweat coating their bodies, Seth nuzzled her collarbone. "Did I hurt you?"

"No, why?"

"It got kind of rough. I'm sorry." Concern for his partner's well-being a first for Seth. His next question triggered another. "Did you enjoy it?"

"Seth, it…it was exquisite. Why the third degree? I'd have stopped you if you were too rough." Natalie's hand on his side branded his flesh.

"I…it's nothing. We have a game tomorrow. I'll go." He pushed away from the couch.

"Stay. Spend the night." Natalie's hand halted his movement, and him staying silent, she added, "We'll just sleep. I promise."

More silence and his expression stiffened.

"What are you afraid of?"

"N-nothing. I…"

"Talk to me." Natalie's heart ached at the indecision etched on his face.

His survival instinct battled his innate honesty. The honesty won, and he corralled his thoughts.

"Seth, just tell me. I won't judge you."

"I've never spent an entire night with a woman."

"That's what's worrying you? We'll just sleep, no sex, but to be honest, I prefer riding the hell out of you." Her eyes twinkled and she cupped him.

"You do?" Seth cursed himself at showcasing his immaturity.

"From the first moment we met."

An unreadable expression greeted her, and she pushed at his chest and wriggled out from beneath him. Her legs swung off the couch, she rose, and clutched his hand. She tugged him upright and led him to the bedroom.

"Quick or drawn out?" A wicked smile surfaced.

HER QUESTION CAUGHT him off guard. None of his past partners cared if he enjoyed the experience and words eluded him.

"Let me love you." Natalie stepped closer and worked the used condom off and disposed of it.

"Yes." The word stuck in Seth's throat.

A hundred questions pestered Natalie. The depth of pleasure Seth evoked contradicted the sexual experience a normal twenty-one-year-old exhibited.

"I'm going to pleasure you, Seth. All of you." Natalie massaged him into a painful hardened erection.

Seth's groin ached from Natalie caressing his extra sensitive pleasure spot. A deep, paralyzing, tightness clenched his rigid flesh and his legs buckled.

"On the bed." Natalie dragged her hands from his groin, and she shoved him in the chest, sending him onto the bed. She pushed his legs apart and crawled between them.

Her hands working their magic, her mouth covered his length. Seth's world shattered around him, his vision darkened, and a sheen of sweat prickled his skin.

He wanted more. This addiction far exceeded his thirst for drugs and Seth clutched her head, preventing her from pulling away.

"Harder, please, please." Seth's begging checked off another on his growing list of sexual firsts.

Natalie released him with a loud pop. Her breath teasing his throbbing flesh. "I'm afraid I'll hurt you."

"I trust you. Please, Natalie. It's so…"

She resumed the exquisite torture, and this time drawing him deeper into her mouth and Seth rolled his hips.

He pleaded again. "Harder." He repeated his request multiple times and Natalie obliged.

A twinge shot through his length, but he ignored it. The tornado of never-experienced pleasure bursting upon him outweighed the momentary twinge. Seth's ecstasy spun him into a foreign universe, and he gulped in air.

Natalie perched herself on Seth's abdomen, and fearful her aggression injured him, she stroked his face.

"Seth. Hey, are you okay?"

She mistook his silence and expression for discomfort. "I'm sorry if I hurt you."

"You didn't." He drew in a breath and opened his eyes. "You gave me something I've…"

"Seth it's okay if you're embarrassed. There's eight years between us."

"It's not my age. It's…" The appropriate words and underlying dread of her judgment left him mute.

"Baby, talk to me. I've never experienced anything like what just happened between us. Never." She paused." Can I go out on a limb and say something?" Natalie drew random patterns on his chest.

"Sure."

"It's okay if you're, uh, not as experienced. You're only—"

Seth's laughter cut her off and she narrowed her eyes.

"I'm sorry. Natalie, you're a cop…and…"

"And what? So, I'm a cop. Why are you laughing?"

Seth's laughter abated and his features hardened. "I prostituted myself to survive. I had no choice."

Natalie gaped, wide-eyed at him. "Okay."

"I'll leave." Seth eased away from her and swung his legs off the bed. Natalie grasping his arm arrested his abrupt departure.

"Stay with me, Seth. Stay the night."

Her soft entreating voice broke his resolve, but he resisted dropping his chin and closing his eyes.

"Please, I want to know you better. I need your strength next to me. You make me feel safe."

The silence lengthened until Seth turned, his gaze finding Natalie's.

"You're a cop. You're not afraid of anything."

This time Natalie laughed and pulled him back on the bed. Her hand covering his heart, she smiled.

"Seth Doyle, I'm afraid of a lot of things. Including my sudden and intense feelings for you."

Truth shone in Natalie's beautiful light brown eyes. He studied them for a long minute and dove into the unknown. His kiss tender and sensual, he wrapped himself around her.

THIS TIME their lovemaking slower and tender. An exploration. A journey of discovery.

Natalie and Seth, bodies entangled, drifted asleep.

CHAPTER 8

The first rays of morning filtered into the bedroom, and Natalie stretched, smiling at the solid, warm body alongside her.

Light continued brightening the room, she stroked the length of Seth's arm. His smooth flesh sparked a fire, and it coursed through her veins and into her core.

Her hand reaching his forearm, she paused. Natalie's trained eyes riveted on the faded track marks, and she raised her chin and studied him.

Seth's eyelids fluttered open. Street life forced him to develop a constant awareness of his surroundings. It meant staying alive. Natalie's scrutiny brought immediate concern and his eyes dropped to her hand on his arm.

"I haven't shot up in twenty-one months"

His earlier revelation, shocking, but now made sense considering his prior drug use. Natalie wasn't blind to an addict's life.

Seth lay silent, waiting for Natalie to speak. A long minute passed, and nothing said, he rolled away from her.

"Seth, stay."

"Why? I can't change my past, and you're a cop."

"My being a cop has nothing to do with this unless we let it. We all have a past, Seth." Natalie shuffled closer and hugged him.

"Mine's bad, really bad, and you deserve a lot better than a former prostituting junkie."

"And how do you know mine isn't?"

Seth cocked his head, his eyes meeting hers. "I don't."

"Look, you have a game tonight, and that's what you need to focus on. We can talk afterward, or whenever you're ready." Natalie smiled and cupped his stubbled jaw.

"I'm the up-front, tell-it-as-it-is, kind of guy, remember?"

"Come on, handsome, you need a good hearty breakfast."

"It can wait." Seth twisted and pressed Natalie into the bed. He slid on a condom, spread her legs, and pushed inside her.

"Oh, Seth. God, you feel good."

Their lovemaking slow and sensual escalated into an animalistic mating frenzy, alternating who rode who until both lay quiet and satiated. Natalie slumped across Seth's chest.

HIS COMPRESSION SOCK half pulled on, Logan paused, and glanced sideways at Seth.

"Enjoy your evening?"

"Yeah, I did." Seth retrieved his shoulder pads and shrugged into them.

"I hear someone's got himself a girlfriend, or are you just banging her?" Brad Myurzz taunted upon his entrance into the locker room and sank onto the bench. His stall next to Seth's.

"Fuck you, Brad." Seth shot a grin at his teammate.

"Hey, man, she's hot. If I wasn't taken, I'd hook up with her."

"I'm not hooking up. I like her."

Brad nodded in approval and nudged Seth. "Good for you."

The subject switched to pre-game talk until Marshall's form filled the doorway.

"Seth."

Seth wedged his stick against his stall and trudged into the hallway, Marshall following. He kept quiet, unsure why his coach summoned him.

"Tonight's opponent, they're fast and good at working the puck inside and getting a lot of shots on goal. We need you focused tonight." Marshall's gaze held Seth's.

"I'm good, Coach."

"Everything okay?"

"Yeah. If you're wondering where I spent last night. I stayed at Natalie's. Moira's friend. She's a cop, Coach. Do you want the details?" Seth smirked and arched his brows.

"Go finish suiting up." Marshall smiled and slapped Seth's back. Seth entering the doorway, he added, "Remember, I'm always here, Seth."

Seth nodded his head. "I know. Thanks, Coach."

Marshall dipped his head, and Seth disappeared inside the locker room.

NATALIE ENTERED THE MILLS' suite and accepted the beer Moira handed her. Her friend wasted no time peppering her with questions.

"Damn, slow down, girl. There are things a lady doesn't reveal."

"Fuck that, Nat. Spill it, girlfriend." Moira's gaze bore into Natalie's, and she tapped her foot.

"Where do I start? With the most exquisite orgasm I've experienced over there." Natalie pointed where Seth pinned her against the boards.

"Okay, again, TMI. I'll come back at puck drop." Cooper u-turned in the doorway.

"Come on, Coop. Stay." Moira pouted and seized Cooper's hands.

"Uh, no. I'll see you at puck drop."

"I've never seen him blush," Moira said, chuckling and nodding at the ice, "and you're pulling my leg on doing it out there, right?"

"No, because shit, he has wonderful hands. It was wicked, Moira."

The two leaning against the counter, Natalie shared the details of the on-ice tryst.

Moira fanned herself, finished her beer, and plucked two more from the refrigerator. "Can you please have him give Cooper some pointers?"

"Yeah, probably not. Look, Moira, I'm assuming Cooper's familiar with Seth's past."

"I guess so, he is the GM. Why?" Moira's brow creased.

"Then he hasn't told you." Natalie sipped her beer.

"Told me what?"

"Sit." Natalie nodded at the bar chairs.

"I'll stand. What's wrong with him?"

"Oh, nothing, other than his super shady, criminal past." Natalie swallowed a large mouthful of beer.

"That's a relief, I was afraid he had a sex change or something." Moira forced a laugh.

"No, he's all male, my friend. All male and some. He's...never mind." Natalie's grin faltered.

"What?"

"He refused kissing me on the mouth at first and considering how he made me feel out there." She waved her hand at the rink. "It was odd."

"That is weird."

"Yeah, no shit. I kept trying, but he kept evading me. So, I called him out on it, and you'll never believe why?"

"Probably not." Moira stiffened, bracing herself. "Nat, I won't say anything."

"Promise. You can't say anything to Seth or Cooper."

"I promise. It's serious, isn't it." Moira bent forward, her hands gripping her beer.

"Yes and no. You know the gut feeling we get at work dealing with perps?"

"Yeah."

"I'm not sure how to handle this because I like him, Moira. I mean I really, really like him." Natalie rested her elbows on the counter and hung her head.

"Nat, just tell me." Moira squeezed Natalie's arm.

"I asked him why he wouldn't kiss me on the mouth, and he didn't answer. He eventually kissed me but… he acted like he'd never kissed a woman before. After we had sex, I asked him to stay the night."

Natalie sipped her beer.

Moira stayed quiet.

"He admitted he never spent the night with a woman. I was okay with that."

"And?"

"He prostituted himself. It shocked me, but I didn't ask him why. I should've."

"Uh, yeah, you need to."

"There's more."

Natalie delayed elaborating, and the awkwardness stretched out.

Moira on the verge of screaming, her best friend's flat tone broke the silence.

"He shot dope in the past. The track marks are faint but there."

"Do you believe him?"

"I do, but I sense there is something else, but I don't know what. We both know it's not uncommon for drug addicts to engage in prostitution. I just can't put my finger on it."

"Nat, if you want a relationship with him, you need answers. You have a right to ask questions," Moira said.

"I know, and he'll tell me, but I want him to do so willingly. I know that sounds crazy, but it's important."

"I can talk to Cooper."

"No. We need to trust each other and from what I've gathered, he's never trusted anyone. Besides, even if Cooper knows anything, he wouldn't be at liberty to tell either of us.

"Hey, ladies. Are we done with…okay, those are serious faces, I'll come back." Cooper entered the suite and his singsong voice dropped.

67

"Nah, you're fine. You want another, Moira?" Natalie indicated the beer cans sitting in a bucket of ice.

"I'm good, thanks."

Cooper sitting next to her, Moira kissed him.

"Are you two, okay?" Cooper snaked his arm around Moira's waist.

"Yeah, we're good. Work talk." Moira hated lying.

The trio settled in for the game.

THE SCORE TIED HALFWAY through the second, Seth positioned himself several feet away from the net. The puck staying in sight, he pivoted at the same time his opponent shot.

Seth twisted, catching the line drive shot in the side. The impact stung and winded him, but he pushed through the pain, and grunting, lunged at the loose puck, passing it to Aleksander.

He kept his eyes on Aleksander racing down the ice and rose to his feet. Seth forced aside his grimace and skated out of his defensive zone.

"DiPaulo, in. Doyle, off," Marshall shouted.

Seth obeyed and stepped into the bench area.

Aleksander fired the puck into the net on the short side and the Patriots' bench jumped to their feet. Marshall noted Seth's clenched jaw.

"Ansley."

Her hand on Seth's shoulder, Ansley leaned forward. "How's your side?"

"I'm good, thanks."

"Okay. Let me know. We'll look at it between periods." Ansley addressed the last to Marshall.

"He says he's fine, but that was a hell of shot in the ribs. I'll assess it further during the intermission."

"Thanks. Kid's tough."

"Or stupid." Ansley smiled.

"No, he's tough."

Marshall held Seth out an extra shift but observing his defense-man's pinched brows, he nodded and his protégé leapt over the boards.

THE BUZZER SOUNDED, ending the second period, and the team filed into the locker room. Seth removed his jersey and shoulder pads and lifted his compression shirt, surveying the bruise.

Ansley poked her head around the door and summoned Seth.

Inside the training room Ansley commenced her examination. Except a mild twitch on Seth's part, he hid his pain, but it didn't escape her.

"Here." Ansley handed him an ice pack.

"Thanks." Seth held the ice on his side. This time he did flinch.

Seth slid off the table and focused on Marshall entering the room.

"Let me see."

Seth removed the cold compress and Marshall inspected the bruise.

"We'll keep an eye on it. No indication of cracked ribs. I'd do precautionary X-rays," Ansley said.

"Coach, I'm good. I've suffered worse. I promise I'll say some-thing if it bothers me. I promise." Seth's puppy dog expression tugged at Marshall's better sense.

"Okay. Alek's goal tied it up. A win will put us in first. This team is our greatest adversary this year." Marshall said and left.

"Let's bind those ribs for precaution, provides extra padding," Ansley said.

His ribs wrapped, Seth shrugged into his shoulder pads and jersey.

THE THIRD PERIOD STARTED, and Seth maintained his regular shifts, ignoring his sore ribs.

Five minutes remained on the game clock and a penalty called on their opponents, granted the Patriots a power play. Marshall opted skating four forwards instead of three, leaving a sole defenseman, Seth.

Logan fed Brad's pass to Seth, and he one-timed the puck from three feet inside the blue line. His shot whizzed pass the goalie's head and slammed into the back of the net with such force it dented the holder for the netminder's water bottle.

Seth threw his arms into the air in celebration, paying no heed to the flash of pain streaking through his ribs.

Brad dug the puck out of the net and dropped it in Seth's hand. Tyler shoved him toward the bench and Seth led the goal celebration line past his teammates. He exited the ice at the opposite end, sat, and admired the puck in his glove.

"Great shot, Doyle."

"Thanks, Coach."

His grin splitting his face, Seth handed the puck to the team's equipment manager, Travis Warrensen for safekeeping.

The game-ending buzzer sounded, and Seth and his jubilant teammates acknowledged the fans and left. Prior to stepping off the playing surface, Seth paused and tilted his head, his eyes on Natalie standing at the counter in the Mills' suite. He lifted his stick and smiled. In return she blew him a kiss and he disappeared into the tunnel.

Showered and on his way to the dressing room, Ansley summoned him into the training room. He checked the towel around his waist and stepped inside.

"How are the ribs?"

"Sore, but I'll live."

"We'll do X-rays."

Twenty minutes later, changed into his street clothes, he left the dressing room. He spied Natalie, Cooper, and Moira at the end of the hallway leading to the players' parking exit door.

"Hey, handsome. Great game. You, okay?" On tiptoes, Natalie brushed her lips across Seth's, smiling at his easy acceptance of the kiss, but she clutched his hands instead of hugging him.

Moira and Cooper bid them goodbye leaving Seth and Natalie alone.

"You can kiss my bruise later and make it better." He indicated his side and draped his arm around Natalie and led her away. "I'm starving."

"For me?"

"Always, but I need food first." Seth kissed the side of her head.

"We can eat out or bring something back."

"Let's do carryout. Oh, and Nat, here." Seth dug into his pocket, pulled out the puck, and placed it in her hand.

"Seth, no. It's your first professional goal. Thank you, but you keep it." She pressed the rubber disc into his palm.

"Nat…"

"Yeah."

"Can it work between us? Marshall says I can make it all the way."

"If we want it to…and I do."

"What about your job? I mean if I make it. I won't be staying here."

"Seth, do you have any idea how much the base salary is for an NHL player? I can find something, but I'd prefer staying home and raising baby Doyles. Besides, there are tons of work-from home jobs." Natalie swatted his side. Her smile dropped the instant her hand connected with his torso. "Shit, I'm sorry."

"It's ok. Let's go." He entangled their fingers, and they left the arena.

CHAPTER 9

Their favorite take-out food in hand, Seth and Natalie entered her apartment. Seth gathered the plates and silverware and Natalie attended Elvis.

The two settled at the table and ate in silence. Elvis stretched out on the floor by Seth, his head trapping Seth's foot.

"He likes me."

"I'd say so. He's a good judge of character. He's saved my butt a few times." A fork full of salad halfway to her mouth, Natalie paused and smiled.

Seth stared at Natalie, a thousand conflicting scenarios tumbling around in his brain.

Natalie lowered her fork and straightened in the chair. "Seth, is my job a problem?"

"No, why? Do you think because of my past, I'm holding it against you?"

"I don't know."

Seth placed his utensil on his plate and met her eyes. "Ask me whatever."

Natalie sucked her lip between her teeth and studied Seth. "What made you stop?"

"Right to the point. You're not curious why I started?"

"Yes, but I can guess why, and in the scheme of things, does it matter?" Natalie kept eye contact.

"True. Can we finish eating first? I hate wasting food."

"Sure." Natalie's smile blossomed.

Finished eating, Seth cleared the dishes and Natalie packaged the leftovers.

No reason to sugarcoat his answer to Natalie's earlier question, Seth said, "I had sex with a girl one night and she overdosed."

A soapy dish in hand, Natalie spun and faced him.

"You asked."

Natalie turned off the water, dried her hands, and propped her hip against the counter. "Seth, were you there when she died?"

"Uh, yeah. I fucked her." A muscle twitched in his jaw, and he glared at her.

"Hey, I wasn't meaning it that way. I'm sorry. What I meant was… shit, how do I say this?" Natalie dropped the towel on the counter.

"Look, we were high. Really high. Tremaine brought us together and told me to show her a good time." Seth paused, the episode a jumbled mess of images. "Honestly, she only cared about getting high. She…just…so, I did her and Tre gave me my next fix."

"Was she alive when you…finished?"

"Yeah, I guess. She was making noises."

"You're one hundred percent sure she died from an overdose?"

The distorted scene rocketed around Seth's head.

"It's all a blur, Nat. I hit up once we finished, but the police kept saying she was murdered."

"Think, Seth. I know it's hard but try to remember. Anything."

Seth scoured his brain, combing through the haze. "Tremaine did her too. We snorted lines and she wanted sex again, but I was too high. She kept begging for someone to do her. It was the drugs. She didn't care who fucked her or even if we did. Tremaine mainlined her and threw her on the floor and demanded I screw her. He wanted her quiet. She went all crazy and flipped out."

Seth paused, but he kept the truth buried. "So, I tried doing her, but we were both stoned. I figured she blacked out. I must have too. The next thing I remember, the cops come sniffing around asking questions. Tremaine said to keep my mouth shut, and I did."

"Did she overdose?"

"You don't believe me, do you?" Seth withheld sharing how rough Tremaine was during his sexual pursuits.

Natalie's hand clutched his arm. "Seth, if Tremaine believes you can tell the cops what happened, he'll—"

"Nat, if I was a threat, he would've killed me already."

"Maybe, maybe not. You're clean and out of Chicago and more of a threat now."

"Come on, you're a cop. They won't believe anything I say. I was fucking high. I'm guessing that's how it happened. I fucked her. The rest is a big blur."

"I know how these people think, work. No one leaves these gangs alive."

"I did. Look, whatever happened, I have no I idea, but it was the pivotal point for me. I stopped using the hard stuff. The withdrawal was hell, Nat. I almost gave in, but that night haunted me, and I wanted to escape that life."

Elvis squeezed between the pair and Seth stroked the dog's fur.

"Okay. I appreciate your honesty but humor me if I worry. Gut instinct is a cop's biggest asset and mine seldom leads me astray. You know more than what you think. You witnessed something horrible, but your mind refuses recalling it." Natalie pressed her hand on his arm.

Seth pulled her against him, resting his chin on the top of her head.

"Nat?"

"Yes."

"Make love to me. I love the way you make me feel."

Natalie ruffled the dog's ears, saying, "Elvis, crate."

The dog obeyed.

Her hands drifted from Seth's cheeks to his shirt. She undid the buttons and pulled it from his pants.

"Sit on the counter."

Seth heeded her command and Natalie stepped between his legs. "Tell me where to touch you."

Her hand palmed his chest. "Here?" The same question preceded each caress until her finger tossed his erect shaft.

"This?"

"Yes."

Natalie eased a hand beneath him, stroking his tender pleasure spot. His hips bucked, and her mouth covered him.

"Nat. God...it feels..."

Seth knotted his fingers into her hair, forcing more pressure on himself. Natalie granted his unspoken request, spiraling him into an exhilarating climax. His guttural moan filled the apartment and his chest heaved from the explosive orgasm.

Natalie straightened and rested her hands on his thighs. Fearful of having injured him, she spoke. "Seth, baby—"

"I'm fine."

"I'm always afraid I'll hurt you."

"You'd never hurt me. Nat, I need to tell you something. I hated it but I...you understand...I had no choice." Seth waited for her condemnation. None came.

"Just tell me Seth."

"I...it wasn't just women." Seth lowered his gaze. "I had no choice, Tre made me do it."

Natalie's mind raced, and the color drained from her face. Her voice froze in her throat.

Seth's eyelids closed and his head drooped. Her silence a stab to his heart and he slid off the counter, dressed, snatched his jacket from the chair, and left.

Natalie's instinct urged her to follow Seth, but her feet refused cooperating.

OUTSIDE NATALIE'S APARTMENT, Seth sat in his SUV, his mind a confusion of emotions. Five minutes passed and he cranked the Cayenne's engine and drove away. He swung the SUV into the gas station near the players' apartment complex. A six-pack of beer in hand, he drove home.

On his journey across the parking lot, he popped the cap off one of the beers and chugged it. He opened a second bottle at the apartment door, shoved it open and stormed to the balcony, polishing off the drink on his way.

"Hey, Seth. Everything okay?" Logan joined him on the balcony.

"Yeah."

"Lady trouble?"

"Kind of."

"I'm here if you need me. If you're hungry, Kimmie made lasagna earlier," Logan said.

"Thanks."

"Sure. Hey, I'm serious. Kimmie and I are both here for you."

"Appreciate it, but I'm good." Seth forced a smile and brushed past Logan. He dumped the empty beer bottles in the trash and disappeared in his room.

"Is he okay?" Kimmie asked Logan.

"He says so but I'm not buying it."

Kimmie frowned. "Something's wrong. I'll call Natalie."

"No, leave it. Come on, it's late." Logan grasped her hand.

TREMAINE and four of his henchmen arrived in Charleston at the same time Natalie pleasured Seth. The gang commandeered the home of one of his henchmen's family members on the outskirts of the West Ashley area.

Their fatigue from the long drive insufficient in deterring them from indulging in drinking, drugs, and sex.

Noontime rolled around, and the partiers stirred. His body entangled with two women, Tremaine shoved them aside, and commanded they leave the bedroom.

Tremaine, half-dressed, strutted into the kitchen, demanded something to eat, and sank into a chair. He grabbed the newspaper laying on the table. The paper itself held no interest, but he flipped to the sports page.

The front-page photo pictured Seth Doyle, his hands in the air, and Tremaine read the accompanying headline.

Patriots' rookie defenseman celebrates first professional goal.

"Enjoy it for now, you motherfucking cocksucker. You're mine. No one leaves Tremaine Kingston. No one, Seth. No one. Not even you."

Tremaine threw the paper onto the table and slammed his fist on the color photograph.

CHAPTER 10

The team traveling home to Charleston, Seth rested his head against the bus window, sleep eluding him. A week passed without any communication between himself and Natalie, and he missed her. The game a physical one, but his muscle aches paled in comparison to the need for the pleasure Natalie induced, and the hurt in his heart.

The Patriots' team bus arrived at the arena at 3:10 am, and Seth, teammates, and staff lumbered off and into the arena. Marshall exited last and followed his team inside.

Seth dawdled placing his equipment into his locker stall, an empty bed waiting at home held no appeal.

He battled his stubbornness, the one trait he employed to ensure his survival prior to leaving Chicago. His former lifestyle mandated he become a realist, and both now kept him from the woman he loved. Despite her occupation, Seth accepted his former lifestyle was too much for Natalie.

Seth left the locker room and peered to his right. The faint glow of light from Marshall's office tempted him to confide in his coach, but aware Aleksander, Natasha, and the two goons monopolized Marshall's time, he decided against adding to his coach's stress.

Outside, he crossed the parking lot. Marshall's newer-model Cayenne parked closer than his, he slowed his pace once he reached the rear of his coach's vehicle. The hairs on the back of his neck prickling, hinting at danger, his senses kicked into high alert, and he squinted into the darkness.

The parking lot's low lighting cast deep, menacing shadows and Seth paused. His gut warned him danger lurked, and he scanned his surroundings, but found no threat.

Despite no longer living in Chicago's intercity he always kept his guard. Goosebumps erupting along his flesh, he turned, and caught the flash of metal.

"Hi, Seth."

Trigs, one of Tremaine's gang members swung his handgun, catching Seth on the right eyebrow. Oblivion descended and Seth slumped to the ground.

"Let's go boys. It's party time." Tremaine urged his cronies inside the waiting van.

"Damn, fucker's heavy." Shivs, another gang member, grunted and struggled helping carry an unconscious Seth.

Seth dumped inside the van, the others climbed in, and the vehicle sped out of the parking lot.

"Slow down you fucking idiot. You want the cops stopping us? Fucking moron," Tremaine waved his hands around and glanced into the rear of the van. "Make sure he's tied tight and shoot him up."

"Fucker has muscle, Tre." Trigs eyed Tremaine.

"No shit, moron. He's playing professional hockey."

The van arriving at their destination, Tremaine preceded his gangsters inside. A flick of his hand and the group conveyed Seth to one of the bedrooms.

"Tre, he's hot." One of the girls living at the house sashayed her way across the room, admiring Seth. She trailed one finger along his body. "Let me have him."

"Later." Tremaine shoved her away.

Trigs and Shiv left Seth on the floor. His ankles secured and his hands tied behind his back, the two circled a rope around Seth's torso, and pinned his arms to his side.

"Wake him up and bring me the heroin. Let's party."

MARSHALL LOCKED his office and trudged through the bowels of the arena. He opened the exit door and stopped. Two Porsche Cayennes remained in the players' parking area. An uneasy chill raced along Marshall's spine.

He surveyed the area but noted nothing abnormal. Marshall shook his head and returned inside the arena.

"Seth."

Marshall cupped his hands and called his young defenseman's name a second and third time. His quick strides carried him to the dressing room and the other adjacent ones, he reverted to his on-ice tone, shouting, "Doyle!"

No answer.

Marshall ducked into the locker room and flipped on the light. He examined Seth's equipment stall, and nothing appeared out of place. He inhaled and made his way to the rink.

No one.

Marshall ignored the time, 3:40 am and dialed Cooper's number. A drowsy hello greeted him.

"Mills. I need Natalie's number. Now."

"What? Marshall, it's frigging—"

"Damn it, Mills this is important." A muscle twitching in Marshall's jaw, he clenched a fist.

"Hold on."

Marshall pacing outside the exit door, he rolled his eyes waiting on Cooper waking Moira.

"Marshall?" Her sleepy voice greeted.

"Moira, I need Natalie's number, or you call and have her call me ASAP."

"Uh, right now? She's working. What's wrong?" Moira's voice sharpened, and concern laced it.

"Yes, right now."

"Marshall, what the hell is going on?" Cooper's question reached through the phone.

"We're on speaker phone. Now tell us what the hell is going on," Moira said.

"I'm not sure but something's wrong. Seth's car is in the parking lot and he's—"

"Did you call Logan, maybe he had car trouble and rode home with someone else," Cooper said.

"No. I'll call him right now."

"We're on our way. I'll call Natalie," Moira said. Her volley of instructions to Cooper reached Marshall before he disconnected the call.

Marshall called Logan. His groggy player answering, he asked if Seth caught a ride with him. Logan's negative answer prompted him asking Logan to check and see if Seth was home. He tapped his foot waiting.

"He's not here, Coach. He's probably at—"

"Thanks, go back to sleep Logan." Marshall ended the call and texted Cooper the news.

One legacy he gained from his four years with the Chicago Police Department was having become adept at keeping his cool and discovering clues, he approached Seth's vehicle with caution.

He made a thorough inspection of the vehicle and the surrounding areas. Nothing. No obvious signs of foul play.

A beam of light from approaching headlights illuminated the rear driver's panel of Seth's Cayenne. Several minuscule dark spots marring the white paint attracted Marshall's trained eyes. He pointed his phone's flashlight at the metal and cursed. The light inadequate in proving his suspicions.

The North Charleston Police Department SUV approaching him, Marshall clicked off the flashlight mode and waited for the vehicle to stop.

"Moira called and told me to hightail it here. What's…is Seth, okay?" Natalie's gaze darted from Marshall to Seth's car parked two spaces away from his coach's.

"I was hoping you'd tell me."

"Seth and…we… haven't spoken in a week."

"Explains his moods, but why? Never mind. What's important right now is where the hell is he?"

"He has a key to my place, but I doubt he's there. Marshall, what if—"

"I'm avoiding those thoughts, Nat, but with his past…"

"Yeah, I know. I should've called him." Natalie offered a condensed explanation behind her and Seth's fall out. "I didn't know what to say, how to react. Odd for my profession, right? I know it happens, but—"

Cooper's Corvette skidding to a stop near her Tahoe, redirected Natalie's words, and she said, "You're suspicious he found someone to supply him drugs."

"I hope not, but what other explanation is there."

"I'm a big girl, Coach. No need to sugar coat your suspicions."

"You are, but love can blind us, Nat." Marshall called Seth's phone.

Cooper and Moira rushing from their vehicle, Moira's eyes darted between Marshall and Natalie. "Anything? Any word?"

Four rings later Seth's voice mail answered, and Marshall left another message.

"Could he have gone home—"

"Cooper!" Moira smacked his arm and cut her eyes at him.

"It's okay." Natalie forced a grin.

Marshall fired off a text.

Natalie walked several feet away from Marshall and Cooper. Moira, having brought her work flashlight, joined her best friend. "Are you okay?"

"Yeah."

"Liar."

Cooper glanced at Marshall.

Marshall sighed and said, "Nothing here, that I can see indicates foul play except that." He indicated the possible blood droplets splattered on Seth's Cayenne.

"Blood?" Cooper stepped closer to the vehicle.

"Possible. Luminol would confirm it," Natalie said

"Then test it." Cooper waved his hand.

"We'd need a crime scene technician," Moira said.

"There's not enough evidence to warrant that." The exasperation in Marshall's voice brought the others facing him.

"Moira. Nat. Can't either of you call in a favor?" Cooper asked.

"Not that easy, Coop and there are more questions than we have answers for right now," Marshall said.

"Well, that's fucked up."

Moira searched around Marshall's vehicle and Natalie freed Elvis from her Tahoe. She kept a loose grip on his leash, letting the dog work the area, guiding him around Seth's Cayenne. Her attention focused on Elvis she asked Marshall, "Can you track your players through their phones?"

"No."

"Maybe he does have a new girl." Cooper shrugged.

Moira's blazing glare brought an immediate apology from him.

"No, no new girl. I consider myself a decent judge of people. The boy is head over heels in love with Natalie."

Elvis sat, and Natalie's heart constricted. "Marshall, there's nothing to justify our—"

"I know, no signs of foul play and he's an adult, but I'd appreciate—"

"Consider it done. I'll pass along the word. Call me if you hear from him. I'll keep calling, and nose around the known drug areas, too, until I'm off."

"Nat. I'm riding with you. Four eyes are better than two," Moira said.

"Thanks."

"Is there anything I can do?" Cooper's attention swung between the other three.

"You can pray he hasn't gone looking for a hit." Marshall met Cooper's gaze.

NATALIE AND MARSHALL exchanged numbers and the two said goodbye. Cooper kissed Moira and headed to his car and drove off. Marshall left not long afterward.

The men's vehicles out of view, Natalie and Moira searched the parking lot a second time. This time extending their perimeter.

Both swung their flashlights in slow arcs, illuminating the ground. On one of the sweeps Elvis tugged on his leash and Natalie followed his track. Moira with her.

Natalie pulled a pair of disposable gloves from her pants pocket, slipped them on, bent, and retrieved a cigarette butt. Her sharp eye, and the discarded stub's odor verified it was a homemade joint.

Elvis' bark added proof.

"Maybe he is back to his old habits."

"No. Seth and I might not have known each other long, but he's not—"

"I'm sorry, Nat. We both know the odds of people coming clean and staying clean."

"I know but Seth's different. He loves hockey, Moira, and he wants out. Totally out. He's determined."

"Then we better figure out what the hell happened and where he is."

"Where are you, Seth? Where did you go? Are you okay? Give me a sign, baby. Give me a sign." Natalie's line of vision traveled around the area, but she found nothing more. Not one concrete clue.

Moira laid a comforting hand on her best friend's shoulder.

Natalie huffed a frustrated breath, and the trio walked to her SUV. She opened the hatch, and dropped the butt into a plastic evidence bag, and Moira secured Elvis inside the truck.

Seated inside her patrol car, Natalie retrieved her phone and dialed Seth's number. Straight into voice mail. She followed the call with a text.

Seth, please call me ASAP.

Natalie made a pass through the arena parking lot but found nothing leading to where Seth went. The two spent the remainder of Natalie's shift making inquiries in the local drug neighborhoods and circling through the arena parking.

Her twelve hours ended, Natalie and Moira hung around the station, speaking to the incoming officers, and passing along pertinent information on Seth. Next, the two contacted the other law enforcement agencies in the area.

Moira dropped off at Cooper's, Natalie detoured to Seth's apartment complex prior to heading home. Nothing.

Natalie parked her patrol vehicle and placed another call to Seth. Voice mail again and she sent another text.

Despite her exhaustion, sleep evaded Natalie. Elvis stretched out on the bed alongside her, but his presence failed comforting her.

"I don't have a good feeling, Elvis." She stroked his ears.

The dog licked her hand and whimpered.

CHAPTER 11

eth's world rotated in a blur around him. The pinching restraints brought an immediate awareness of his bondage.

Voices penetrated his foggy mind. He must be dreaming. The last time he experienced these sensations...*where was he?*

"Hello, Seth."

"Fuck." Seth groaned, and caught a glimpse of Tremaine gesturing, and two people hauled him to his knees.

"T-Tre..." Seth shook his head, counteracting his cloudy vision.

"You forgot lesson number one, Seth. *No one* leaves me." Tremaine closed the distance between them and kicked Seth in the stomach.

"F-fuck...y-you."

"Oh, there'll be fucking. I guarantee it." Tremaine squatted and grasped Seth's chin. "Feeling good? Yeah, you are."

"F-fu..." Seth's body collapsed.

"Let's party." Tremaine stood, chucked a box of condoms on the bed, and waved at the girls. "Have at him, babes."

SETH'S HEAD POUNDED. Music boomed in the distance. A smoky haze enveloped the room, and the sickening aroma of marijuana teased his nostrils. Cool air caressed his nude body.

He forced open his eyelids, and a jackhammering pain drilled his right temple.

Seth tugged on his restraints, but the zip ties held strong. His movements brushed himself against a body, and jerking away, he collided into another. Limp bodies surrounded him, and he focused on his surroundings.

He struggled freeing and repositioning himself but failed. A woman crawled on top of him, her mouth smothering his.

"Get the fuck off me."

"Be nice, Seth," Tremaine said, standing next to the bed.

"Fuck you, Tre." Seth's squirming a vain effort in dislodging the woman.

"Now, now. You know how the game's played." Tremaine's gaze collided with Seth's.

"No." Seth rolled right and left, flipping the girl off him. Another's hand groping at his groin, he angled his legs and knocked it aside. His one knee connecting with her face.

"Play nice, Seth." Tremaine landed two punches on Seth's jaw, cementing his warning. "Leave us." He ordered the girls. "Seth needs a reminder of the rules. Boys."

Seth grunted, twisted, and kicked to break free and escape the beating, instead it triggered additional blows.

"Fucking, shoot him up." Tremaine's glare bore into Seth. "You're learning a lesson, you motherfucking cocksucker."

"No." Seth's struggles knocked the needle out of Trigs' hand.

A knee struck Seth's groin twice, ending his fighting.

"His ass is mine." Tremaine whipped his belt out of his pants and swung it at Seth. The buckle struck him numerous times, leaving welts and scratches.

His assailants pinned him facedown on the floor and Trigs injected the drugs into him. The narcotics coursing into his bloodstream rendered him helpless against becoming someone's whore.

Tremaine initiating his assault, Seth succumbed to the drug induced euphoria.

"HEY, SETHY BOY." Tremaine patted Seth's cheek. "Come on, wake up. This party is just startin'." Seth slow in responding, he punched him. "Come on, there we go. Open those baby blues."

Tremaine's gloating, fuzzy face peering at him, Seth's aim was true, and he spat in his captor's face, uncaring of the repercussions.

"Oh, you'll fucking pay for that." Tremaine slugged Seth in the mouth, splitting open his lip.

"Go ahead, fuck me again. I don't care. It's nothing."

"No. You're sucking my dick, like old times. The way I taught you."

"Fuck you, Kingston. Fuck you."

"Listen here, boy. You do what I say, or I pump you so fucking high with dope you'll never break free. And you'll be whoring yourself on the streets again. Got it."

Seth raised his chin and stared at his captor. "Why? What am I to you?"

Tremaine grinned.

"You." He tapped Seth's chest. "Are a money maker. My best male whore. You're in demand, Seth, and this game of yours ends now. You're costing me tons of money. Now it's payback time. So, you and me, we're coming to an agreement." Tremaine straightened.

"I'll tell them."

Tremaine laughed. "Sure, you will. You were too fucked to remember shit but just in case." He cocked his head and Shivs and Trigs hurried to them. "Put him on his knees." Tremaine left the room, returning with a needle in his hand.

He dropped his pants and sank onto the bed, the needle next to him. Tremaine spread his legs and dangled the needle in front of Seth.

"Take it Seth. You *want* it. *Need* it."

"No." Seth's breathing labored, and his body and mind waged an internal battle.

"Then suck my dick."

"No."

"Bring him closer." The point of the needle pricked Seth's neck.

A kick in Seth's kidney curbed his fight. Defeated, his chin dropped.

"You're choice, Seth." Tremaine nodded and one of his men kicked Seth from behind. The blow dropped Seth into Tremaine's lap.

"Okay. Okay."

Tremaine handed the needle off, and grasping Seth's head, he held it against his groin. "Good. Do me, Seth."

Seth hesitated.

"Now, Seth. You're trying my patience, and if you even consider fighting me, we'll grab your bitch cop and fuck her to death, literally. Now be a good boy and do me like I taught you."

Seth having no choice, he complied.

"Oh, yeah…that's good. Yeah, that's it. Oh, yeah. Fuck yes." Tremaine's satisfaction obtained he shoved Seth away. Their eyes clashing, he grinned. "So damn good. Now do the others."

"No."

"Your choice." Tremaine nodded at Trigs, and he injected Seth, the demon flowing into him.

The delirium from the opiates hitting him, Seth jolted backward and slumped onto the floor. "Y-you…f-fu…fuc…you."

"Go ahead boys. He's all yours." Tremaine dressed and snatched a bag of pills from the dresser and tossed them at Shivs. "Make sure, Seth enjoys the party. I'll send the chicks back in. Do whatever the fuck you want with him."

SETH DESCENDED INTO OBLIVION. Faint voices echoed around him. The influence of the narcotics stole his fighting abilities or denying his tormentors' wishes. Time lost all meaning, and he floated in and out of consciousness, swallowed into the bliss of intoxication.

CHAPTER 12

His assailants having forced pills down Seth's throat at the house, and the high from the drugs dulled the impact of him tumbling out of the moving vehicle. The rough pavement ripped through his shirt sleeves. His entire body hurt, and his lungs burned each time he breathed.

Dumped in the arena parking lot next to his Cayenne, Seth lay in a heap on the cold ground. His limbs failing, he collapsed numerous times levering himself off the ground.

Several more tries and he made it to his hands and knees. His head spinning, he teetered, and face planted into unyielding metal.

Disoriented, he cursed, spat out globules of blood, and squinted.

Seth grimaced, and balanced on his haunches, ignoring the blood dripping from his mouth. Weak and unsteady, he extended his arm, grimacing in pain, he clutched the door handle. He grunted and dragged himself upright, his body slamming into the SUV. Seth swaying on his feet and braced himself against the vehicle.

Blood smeared the white paint from his struggles.

His head resting against the vehicle, he rummaged in his pocket, found the remote and pressed it until the car unlocked. It relocked from his delay in entering and he hit the remote again. This time he pulled on the door handle. The effort of gaining entry left him gasping, and he slumped across the center console.

Unaware of how much time passed, Seth righted himself and pushed the button on the fob, releasing the key and he inserted it in the ignition.

His brain battling for coherence it warned him he was in no condition to drive, but he cranked the engine, put the vehicle in drive, and drove to Natalie's apartment.

SETH STEERED the Cayenne to a cockeyed halt in an empty parking space and placed his hand on the door handle, but kept it closed.

He stared at the plastic bag secured to his forearm. His fingers shaking, he ripped it off, and tore open the bag, grabbing the needle.

"No." His craving overriding his addled senses, he placed the syringe between his teeth and twisted the strips of tape, forming a rope.

His hands trembling in his haste, he tied the two strips together, creating one long cord. He secured the makeshift tourniquet around his arm and pressed the needle into a vein in his hand. Scar tissue having formed in the old injection sites on his arm, his hand provided the easier option.

Sweat dripped from his forehead and into his eyes. He blinked, focusing on the syringe, and his need. His thumb on the plunger he pushed it forward.

A flash of light illuminated the Cayenne's interior and Seth yanked the needle from his arm and flung it away, ignoring the blood running down his hand and arm. He leaned back, his chest heaving.

He ignored the piercing pain each time he breathed. The feud waging in his mind a thousand times worse. His body desperate for the drug's ecstasy, but he spurned the devil who ruled his youth.

HER SHIFT OVER, Natalie yawned, and drove home. Thirty-six hours ago, Seth disappeared, and she'd barely slept. She spent hours scouring the known drug areas, and nothing.

Off the next two days, she intended searching further.

Behind her, Elvis sprang to his feet, barking.

"Yeah, we're home, boy." Natalie cocked her head at Elvis behind the cage separating the front and rear of the SUV.

The dog whined and pawed at the door, barking again.

"Hey, boy, calm down."

His whining persisted and parking the SUV, Natalie released her dog. The leash in hand, Elvis bound past her, and she clipped air. His unexpected bolt sent her stumbling.

"Elvis. Heel." The dog ignored her. Natalie repeated the command, but failed halting him from his intent.

Natalie swore and followed, issuing commands. He continued ignoring them and her frustration grew. On the verge of shouting another directive, it caught in her throat once she observed the rear of a white Porsche Cayenne. Her flashlight in the patrol car, she cursed again, and dropped her hand to her gun.

Elvis pawed the driver's door.

Natalie removed her weapon and eased alongside the vehicle. Her body against the car, she peered into the cargo area and rear seats.

Nothing.

Her angle of sight provided a view of the motionless individual in the driver's seat. Natalie's gaze traveled to the driver's door and the blood smeared across it and the window.

Natalie knocked on the window. No response. She knocked a second time and ordered the person to open the door. Again, no response.

She grabbed the door handle and pulled, swinging it wide, she aimed her gun at the sole occupant.

"Hands on the steering wheel."

No reaction.

Elvis wedged himself between her and the vehicle's driver, his paws on the driver's leg.

"Elvis, heel."

The dog obeyed but stayed between Natalie and the man in the vehicle.

A DOG BARKING pierced Seth's stupor. His body craving the rapture, begged for another hit.

Cold air swept inside the vehicle, but the heaviness of his eyelids prevented him from opening them. A familiar voice ripped him from his delirium.

"N-Nat?"

"SETH?" Her back against the open door, she gaped at the occupant.

Elvis whined and rested his head on Seth's thigh.

"H-hey, boy. N-Nat, help me, please." Seth's trembling hand stroked the dog.

Natalie holstered her gun. "Fucking, Christ, Seth."

She edged around Elvis, slid her arm around Seth, and helped him out of the car. The pavement looming below them, Natalie bore Seth's deadweight and the two trudged across the parking lot. Elvis padded behind them.

She propped Seth against the doorframe and rummaged for her house keys. Once inside, she deposited him on the couch. His head smacked the wall, and Natalie gritted her teeth.

A light switched on provided Natalie her first clear indication of what happened to Seth.

"Fucking shit." Natalie scrutinized his bloodied face, disheveled appearance, and torn clothing. He reeked of marijuana, alcohol, blood, and sex, but her main concern, his physical injuries.

Elvis stretching out on the couch, his paws on Seth's thigh.

Seth rested his hand on the dog's body.

"N-Nat. I-I…I'm sorry. I…"

"Seth, shh, don't talk. We need to clean you up."

"I...I'm high. I...made...me. M-Marsh...sorry." Seth's eyelids dropped and he slumped on the couch until his head lay on a cushion.

"I'll call Marshall. You need medical attention." Natalie perched on the edge of the couch alongside Elvis.

"No...hos..pi...tal, please."

"No promise, Seth, I'm sorry. I'll be right back. Elvis. Stay. Watch." Elvis' ears cocking snagged a hint of a grin from Natalie.

Her phone in hand, Natalie headed to the bathroom. She dialed Marshall's number and collected washcloths.

Marshall answering, she said. "Hey, Seth's here. He's hurt, and high." She conveyed her address and disconnected.

"Marshall is on his way. He's calling Ansley and Neil." Natalie dumped the washcloths on the coffee table and disappeared in the kitchen, returning with two bowls. One empty and one filled with warm water.

"Seth?"

"Hmm."

Natalie swallowed an inaudible sigh of relief. His weak response a sign he remained conscious.

"Let's clean you up, okay?"

"K."

Elvis relinquished his place on the sofa but planted himself on the floor between Seth's legs. His head back on Seth's thigh.

"He's worried about you, and so am I. Can you talk? Tell me what happened." Natalie soaked a washcloth in the water, rung out the excess, and cleaned away the dried blood from his head and face.

Her heart tightened in her chest. She expected him to flinch from the pressure she applied to his mouth and cheek, but he stayed rigid.

Natalie's gaze landing on the deep bruising around his right eye, she grimaced and studied the gash above it. She noted the beads of fresh blood where she already cleaned.

She pressed a fresh damp cloth against the laceration. "Seth, can you hold this? Please, baby, it'll help stop the bleeding."

He succeeded for half a minute. "S-sorry. N-Nat. I tried. I-I said... no. M-made...me."

"I know, baby. I know. What did they give you?"

"H-heroin. Pills. Arm. H-hurts." He lifted his arm with the tourniquet.

"Shit." Natalie leaned across him. His cringe brought an apology from the contact with his torso. She tugged at the tape knotted around his arm. Unable to undo it she withdrew her utility knife.

The tape cut, she inspected the resulting bruise.

"Seth, baby, did you shoot up?" Natalie cleaned the puncture wound and examined the rest of his arms.

"Th-the-n-neck. I-I wanted...to...but I...couldn't....want it...so bad." Seth waved a listless hand at the side of his neck.

"I know, baby. I know."

The doorbell ringing, Natalie answered it, admitting Marshall.

"Neil and Ansley are on their way." Marshall carried a kitchen chair into the living room, placed it next to the couch and sat. "Seth, you'll be okay. We'll protect you."

Seth met his coach's concerned gaze. "C-coach, I...I-m sorry. I coul...couldn't stop..."

The doorbell chimed again. This time Ansley and Neil entered.

"Shit." Neil shoved past Natalie and dropped on the sofa alongside his patient. During his initial examination, he barked off several instructions.

Natalie led the way to the bedroom and Ansley followed, a medical bag in hand. Marshall assisting Neil, the two transferred Seth to the bedroom.

Ansley waited outside and Marshall and Neil helped Seth undress.

Each of the trio swore once they noted the massive bruises, welts and cuts covering Seth's body. Natalie's the loudest and most profound.

Seth settled into the bed, Natalie summoned Ansley.

Ansley attending Seth's facial wounds, Neil inspected his arm.

No noted adverse effects from the tourniquet, Neil asked, "Seth? Hey, buddy. What pills did they give you? How much? How often? Seth, Seth, it important. I'll do a full physical exam and Ansley will stitch the wound above your eye, okay."

"Fen…fentanyl…and heroin. Main…lined."

"There are four injection sites in his neck," Ansley said. She dug inside the medical bag and pulled out a needle and thread.

"C-coach." Seth tipped his head toward Marshall. "I-I'm s-sorry. I c-couldn't…fight."

"Seth, it's okay." Marshall glanced at Neil. "The gash above his eye looks bad. Pistol whipped?"

"My guess, yes, and I wouldn't rule out a concussion," Neil stated during his examination of Seth's upper body. His assessment finished, he added, "He may have a broken rib or two. I'm hoping they're bruised. He needs X-rays, Marshall."

Marshall studying Seth, he shook his head. His desire to personally throttle those responsible for his defenseman's condition overwhelmed him but he kept calm. "A hospital is too risky right now, Neil. He'll be too vulnerable there." Marshall studied Seth.

"Natalie, can he stay here?" Marshall met her eyes. Her anger evident in them and on her face.

"Really? I'm not letting him out of my sight, but his car needs processing."

"I prefer keeping this under the radar until he's more coherent."

"He'll go through withdrawal and have cravings," Neil said, keeping his voice low.

"You…don't need…to whisper. I know they fucked me up."

"We're figuring out a game plan, baby."

"It shouldn't…be as bad. I…did what Tre told me to." Seth's speech becoming less slurred and his vision clearing, he steeled himself for their condemnation. None came.

"Seth, what—" Neil started to ask.

"Sex. I had to. It…kept me…If I didn't, they'd give me more drugs." Seth's voice became stronger the more he talked.

"Seth, please rest." Natalie stroked his arm.

"It's okay. It happened, Nat. I…did what I needed to. It was a better alternative than…" His voice faded, but his eyes stayed on hers.

"It's okay, baby. None of this is your fault. We'll find them. Every one of them." Natalie leaned closer and kissed his jaw.

"Coach?" Seth met Marshall's eyes. "Kingston killed the girl. He strangled her."

CHAPTER 13

O nce Seth fell asleep, the other four gathered in the hallway.

"I'm not letting these guys get away with this." Natalie glanced into the bedroom, reassuring herself Seth remained comfortable and asleep.

"One of us needs to stay," Ansley said.

"I'll stay," Neil said.

"Neil, you're sure?" Marshall studied his friend.

"I'm good. It'll be good doing something useful, and Ansley's right, one of us needs to stay and watch Seth."

"Natalie let's go have a look at Seth's vehicle," Marshall said.

"Call me, if I'm needed sooner, otherwise I'll stop by later," Ansley said and bid the others goodbye.

"I can make a few calls. My guys will keep this quiet the best they can, but you know once they start asking, word will get around," Natalie said.

"I know. How much of Seth's past did he tell you?" Marshall held open the front door and followed Natalie outside.

Natalie shared what Seth told her. The two stopped at the rear of Seth's Cayenne and Natalie placed her phone call. Daylight having brightened the parking lot, Natalie and Marshall inspected the vehicle.

Without touching the SUV, Marshall peered through the passenger front window seat. "There's a needle on the floor. Looks full but it's hard to tell without a closer look."

"Coach, what Seth said about Kingston. What's your take?" Natalie eyed Marshall.

"He witnessed a murder, but either didn't realize it until now, or he did but chose staying quiet out of fear and knowing the word of an addict holds little weight." Marshall stepped away from the vehicle and the two discussed their game plan for the immediate future and keeping Seth safe.

Two narcotics officers from Natalie's department arriving, the duo documented the scene, and bagged the discarded needle.

Marshall's phone rang and noting the caller, Logan Kennedy, he answered. His posture stiffening from the news, he disconnected the call, and faced the other three. "There's a package addressed to Seth at his apartment. Logan found it outside the door."

"Coach, if he witnessed her murder, why didn't Kingston just kill him? There's more to this." Natalie surveyed the area, searching for anything, anyone out of the ordinary.

"We'll talk to Seth. Can someone retrieve the package?" Marshall asked.

"Yeah, no problem." One of the officers nodded and headed off.

His colleague, Eric Douglas, stayed behind and accompanied Natalie inside the apartment.

A late-morning team practice required Marshall's presence and he left.

Seth jolted awake, bathed in sweat, and accepted a towel from Neil.

"I'll be fine. You don't have to stay."

"Seth, I'm here, you're not going through this alone."

"Th-thanks." Seth gritted his teeth against the pain in his abdomen. "What I want—"

"You're not getting it."

Seth forced a smile and dragged the towel across his forehead.

"Hey, careful with your stitches. You'll piss off Ansley if you undo her stitchery." Neil smiled and lifted Seth's hand away.

"I'm not a piece of lace, Neil." Seth stiffened, clenching his teeth, and squeezing his eyes shut

"I know. Look, try and rest. You know you're in for a rough couple of hours." Neil rested his hand on Seth's arm.

"I want, Nat. Please, get her."

"I'll be right back." Neil rose and left the room, colliding into Natalie. "Seth wants you. The withdrawal is starting."

Neil followed Natalie into the bedroom.

"HEY, BABY. YOU, OKAY?" Natalie perched on the edge of the bed.

"Better, now that you're here." Seth's smile a brief one.

Seth drew in several deep breaths, the wave of pain easing. His eyelids opening, he met Natalie's gaze. "I'm sorry, Nat. I shouldn't have come here."

"Nonsense, I've been sick to my stomach since you disappeared. We all have. We'll do this together." Natalie cupped his clammy cheek.

"I don't deserve you, or any of this."

"Seth, we're here for you. You have a bright, successful future ahead of you," Neil said, and handed Natalie a dry towel.

"Do I?"

"Yes, baby, you do. Please, believe that. Marshall Reeves doesn't go out on a limb for someone he doesn't believe in. You'll play in the NHL, baby, whether its Boston or another team." Natalie instilled a no-nonsense tone into her voice.

"You'll be there with me?" Seth grasped her hand. Another sharp pain hitting, he tightened his grip.

"I'll be there. Elvis too."

The dog, having stretched out alongside Seth earlier, rose, and licked him.

"Glad he doesn't hate me."

"Nah, he's a good judge of character." Natalie chuckled.

Seth's free hand stroking Elvis' flank diverted his mind from the pain and the cravings.

"Fuck, I want—"

"No, Seth. You don't." Natalie pressed her leg against his and squeezed his fingers.

Elvis whimpered and directed soulful eyes at Seth.

"You're my drug of choice, Nat. Making love to you is the best high."

"Oh." Red stained Natalie's cheeks.

Flustered, Neil rose from his chair. "I, uh hear coffee calling. I'll text Ansley with an update. There's not much we can do now but wait until this runs its course."

"I'm staying with him."

Seth's arm wrapped around Natalie, and he pulled her close. He ignored the pressure of her lithe body resting on his aching ribs.

"Seth."

"Nat. I'm not dead. Kiss me. Touch me. Please."

Natalie stared at him, unsure.

"It's okay. I understand."

"Seth, I want to kiss you, to touch you, love you, but it'll wait." Natalie tilted his chin, compelling eye contact.

"You're sure? Even knowing…"

Natalie stared at Seth, speech eluding her, and the silence stretched out.

"I'm sorry I didn't call. I…I know what happens in a junkie's world, but I guess…I didn't want to—"

"Believe I did it? I had no choice. I guess I did maybe at first, but I didn't. I did what I needed to survive, Nat. When I did drugs, I didn't care. Sex was nothing but a means of getting my next hit. Then…I kicked it but I…" Seth's gaze never wavered.

"Seth, there's no need to explain."

"Yes. Yes, I need to. I never liked it. Sex was just acts, nothing more, no pleasure. Nothing. Until you." Seth cupped Natalie's cheek. "You…damn. My addiction to you is worse than it was for the drugs. I crave your touch, Nat. Your kisses. The way you touch me."

"Seth, I—"

His hand on her nape, he captured her mouth.

"Love me, Nat. I *want you*."

Natalie eased away from him but kept eye contact. "No, Seth. It's not because I don't want to, or am scared to, but you're injured. I'll stay here next to you if you want."

"Nat—"

"Don't make me go into cop mode." Natalie raised her eyebrows.

Seth stared at her, but she refused backing down. "Will you go into cop mode once I'm better and do a pat down?"

"Well," she paused, "I guess. Now, please rest."

Sleep eliminated any further arguments on Seth's part.

Natalie's exhaustion from working a twelve-hour shift and discovering Seth here tugged her toward sleep and she made her way to the other side of the bed.

Unsure what woke her, Natalie propped herself on her elbow and examined the deep bruises and cuts peppering Seth's face and cringed. She hated admitting, in a rugged way, they enhanced his handsome features, and she soaked in his chiseled chest muscles. She traced each scratch marring his upper body.

His breathing remaining steady and even, she eased off the bed and tiptoed out of the room.

"COFFEE'S COLD." On the receiving end of Natalie's death glare, Eric chuckled.

"Yeah well." Natalie poured a cup and heated it in the microwave. She glanced at Neil. "He's fine. We didn't."

"Do I look worried?"

"On a serious note. The substance in the needle tested positive for heroin," Eric said.

"Not surprising. Any news on the package?" Natalie removed her coffee and sipped it.

"Yeah. Various drug paraphernalia, heroin, and pills."

"Is this guy stupid?" Natalie placed the cup on the table and paced.

"Doubt it. More like fu—arrogant. Sorry, Neil."

"Hey, don't apologize, swearing is a common occurrence with hockey players."

Eric smiled and continued speaking. "Look, Nat, I spoke with Kirk Darby over at DEA and he called their Chicago office. Tremaine Kingston is one bad dude. He runs Chicago's number one drug ring, the Kingstonians. The word is no one leaves Kingston. If Seth did witness the girl's murder, we know how this will end." Mac's gaze followed Natalie.

"What if Seth testifies against him?" Natalie retrieved her coffee but stayed standing.

"He's not a reliable witness." Eric shrugged.

"Marshall needs to have a say in this," Neil added.

"Isn't it my choice?"

Three sets of eyes swung to Seth propped against the corner of the hallway wall.

"Seth. Why are you out of bed?" Natalie discarded her cup on the counter and hurried to him.

"I'm fine. I've been worse, trust me."

"How are your ribs?" Neil joined Natalie at Seth's side.

"They hurt. Can I have something to eat?"

"Uh, yeah, sure. You're hungry?" Natalie hooked her arm around his waist.

Eric jumped out of his chair and helped her guide Seth to a chair.

"Yeah. Last time I ate was after the game. How long was I gone?"

"About thirty-six hours," Neil supplied.

"Fuck, no wonder I'm starving." Seth lowered himself into the chair, thanking and greeting Eric, and Natalie rummaged through the cabinets.

CHAPTER 14

M arshall parked his Cayenne alongside Seth's, accessed the hands-free phone option, and called Casey Taylor, engaged to his best friend Brett Lakovic.

"Hello," a female voice answered.

"Casey, Marshall Reeves."

"Hey Marshall. Are you in town?" Casey, a Boston Police officer greeted.

"No. I need a favor," Marshall said, focusing on a vehicle crawling through the parking lot.

"Sure. Fire away."

"Holston Karz's phone number." Marshall removed a notepad from the center console.

"Okay. Want me to text it? Everything okay?"

"Text is fine and no."

"Uh, okay. Tell me what's going on."

He trusted Casey and disclosed why he wanted Holston's number.

Marshall became acquainted with Karz when the former Army special operative acted as Brett's bodyguard until the authorities caught the individual responsible for stalking and terrorizing his best friend.

He needed Holston's unique abilities and background.

"Damn, Marshall. You're sure he's worth the trouble?" Casey said.

"Yes."

FORTY MINUTES later Marshall disconnected his call with Holston, exited his Cayenne, and observed his surroundings. Steps from Natalie's apartment breezeway, motion in the parking lot caught his eye, and he ducked into the shadows.

Marshall paused and stared at the flashy black SUV parked at the end of the lot and the hooded figure leaping inside. He retrieved his phone and called Boston's top defenseman, a former teammate, and good friend, Colin Montoya. Colin's cousin, the person responsible for putting Casey in touch with Holston.

"Hey, Reeves." The Canadian's accent rang through his phone.

"I need a favor. A big favor."

"Name it."

Marshall concluded his conversation with Colin and texted Natalie.

We have visitors.

NATALIE'S abrupt departure to her bedroom alerted Eric, Neil, and Seth.

Eric rose from his seat, and unholstered his weapon.

Elvis assumed an alert stance.

"Guard." She nodded at Seth and Elvis barked once and she positioned herself at the window adjacent the door.

"Nat, what's going on?" Neil stiffened in his seat.

Eric joined her.

"Marshall spied visitors. You two stay put." She pointed at Neil and Seth.

"Tre is too smart to do anything in broad daylight." Seth followed the pair into the living room.

"I told you to stay in the kitchen with Neil." Natalie glared at him.

"Nat. I'm—"

"Seth, listen to me." Natalie closed the distance between them.

"Think. This is super important and be honest. Did you *see* Kingston kill the girl or are you just assuming he did? It's vital."

"Yes, that's why I shot up so bad afterward. Hoping it erased what I saw. He strangled her. I have no idea why."

"That explains why he wants to keep a hold on you," Eric said.

"What's the big deal, he left Chicago." Neil joined the conversation.

"He pimped me out to regulars. My leaving cost him a lot of money and I witnessed him killing that girl. I was trying to break away from him when I met Marshall."

"Nat. I'm going out the back. Neil, can I borrow your coat?" Eric repositioned his holster to the middle of his back and shoved his badge inside his front pants pocket.

"Uh, sure." Neil gestured at his coat draped over one of the living room chairs.

Eric shrugged into Neil's coat and slipped out of the apartment, unobserved, through a side window.

"Uh, so, how do we keep him safe?" Neil pointed at Seth.

"No idea." Natalie motioned Seth to the window. "You recognize that flashy Caddy?"

"Yeah, that's Kingston's." Seth peered through the glass at the black Cadillac Escalade slowing near his Cayenne.

The vehicle circled through the complex two times and drove off.

Eric reentered the apartment five minutes later.

"Let me guess, Illinois plates? Seth said it's Kingston's." Natalie rolled her eyes.

"Yup. A driver, front passenger, and at least one more in the back. I'm guessing more."

"Trigs, Shivs, and Ice are with him. No idea who the others at the house were," Seth said.

"Do you know their real names?" Eric asked.

"Sorry."

"Seth, you're exhausted. Go rest, please." Natalie's tone commanding.

"I'm fine."

"She's right," Neil said.

"Don't shelter me, Nat." Seth held Natalie's gaze.

"Please go rest. I'll be there in a few." Natalie kissed his cheek, and she urged him to the bedroom.

THE DOORBELL INTERRUPTED the trio's conversation, and Natalie and Eric drew their guns.

Eric shooed Neil into the hallway and followed Natalie, the pair positioning themselves on either side of the front door.

Natalie peaked through the peep hole.

"Nat, it's me." Marshall's voice boomed from the other side of the door.

Marshall admitted inside, he locked the door, and Eric and Natalie holstered their weapons.

"We'll have a bodyguard by midnight." Marshall brushed past the two, and eyed Neil standing at the corner of the kitchen and hallway.

"He's laying down." Neil's voice chased Marshall, halting him at the bedroom. "I texted Ansley and told her we're good for the night."

"Thanks, Neil. You're still okay staying? You know you're in danger being here, right?" Marshall studied Neil.

"I'm not leaving. I'll stay until Natalie kicks me out. His ribs are my main concern until we can get X-rays."

Marshall and Neil joined Eric and Natalie in the kitchen, and seated, Marshall informed the others of Holston Karz's imminent arrival. He shared Karz's background, including his U.S. Army special forces training, and serving four years with the ENATTF, the European Nations Anti-Terrorist Task Force team. Marshall also summarized Holston's bodyguard role for Brett during his stalker incident.

"I'll talk with the guys. We can help shadow Seth." Eric checked his watch, and noting the time, texted his partner.

"Eric, take Seth's car. I've no doubt Kingston and his cronies will put a tail on it," Marshall said.

"Won't that spark their suspicion?" Neil asked.

"Yes, but we want them on edge," Marshall replied.

"They'll be more obvious here. They're on unfamiliar turf," Eric said.

Seth's appearance and his ashen face halted the groups conversation.

"Seth." Neil rose from his seat.

"What's wrong." Natalie's chair crashed to the floor.

"I'm okay."

"Yeah, right." Natalie's arm circled his waist, and he cringed.

"Marshall, he needs a hospital," Neil said, eyeing his friend.

"I know, Neil, but it's too dangerous until Karz arrives," Marshall said.

"They're bruised not broken. I've busted ribs before. They're—"

"That's for a doctor to determine," Neil said.

"I threw up." Seth rested against the wall.

"You should've eaten liquids first." Neil assisted Seth to the couch, and Elvis stretched out alongside him.

"I'll catch you all in the morning. Nat, call if you need us," Eric said, and bid them goodbye.

THE FOURSOME, seated in the living room blanketed in silence, Seth tipped his head against the couch.

Perched on the edge next to him, Natalie held his hand.

"Coach, what do I need to do?"

"Right now, nothing but heal."

CHAPTER 15

wo weeks later, the team doctor, Skip Rushton, cleared Seth to skate, but required him to wear a non-contact jersey during practice. Their morning skate finished, Seth showered, dressed, and headed to Marshall's office.

Seth peeked his head inside. "Coach?"

"Hey, Seth. Come on in. Everything okay?" Marshall gestured at a chair.

"Uh, yeah, kind of. You mind?" Seth nodded at the door. Marshall inclined his head, and Seth closed it, and sat.

"Coach. You know what I did in the past. I…uh, this last situation with Tremaine and the kidnapping. I…uh…I…I always used protection. I…"

"Seth. Just—"

"I'd like to get tested for STD's." Seth twisted in his seat.

"Okay. It's probably a good idea. I'll have Skip make the arrangements. Other than recovering from the injuries, have you been feeling, okay?" Marshall rested his elbows on the desk and steepled his hands together.

"Yeah. I want to make sure for Natalie's sake. I like her Coach. I mean really like her."

"Okay, let me call Skip and set it up." Marshall hit the speed dial on the desk phone for the team doctor. Skip answering on the second ring, Marshall explained the reason for his call.

Marshall thanked the doctor, ended the call, and wrote out an address. "Go straight there and they'll draw your blood and send it off. They'll put a rush on the testing. In the meantime—"

"I know, Coach. Thanks, I better go." Seth rose and opened the office door.

"Seth."

He turned.

"That was gutsy."

"Not really, Coach. It's a fact of life with my past."

"You love her, don't you?"

"Yeah, Coach. I do."

"She's a good one. Remember one thing. Always talk, Seth. Lauren and I lost a lot of time together because we didn't talk." Marshall held Seth's gaze.

"Sometimes, fate has other plans for us, Coach. And when you love someone, you do what is best for them. I'm making this work with Natalie. I got to go." Seth waved the paper.

"Yeah. Don't let your guard down. Karz is shadowing you but be careful."

"I will, Coach. I survived this long." Seth smiled again and left.

Marshall stepped outside his office, his eyes on Seth until he disappeared.

"Yeah, you have kid, and I'm keeping you alive for a lot longer."

SETH PARKED his Cayenne and crossed the lot. Despite Holston shadowing him, he remained vigilant. The apartments within the complex housing the Patriots' players backed against a wooded area providing ample hiding places for intruders.

"Doyle, where you been?" Shivs and Trigs entered the breezeway from behind the building.

"That's none of your business."

"Yeah, well, Tre says it is and we're here to collect payment or…" Shivs gripped Seth's wrist.

Trigs the weaker of the two, and leery of Seth's strength, kept an adequate distance from them, but said, "Come on man, don't make us do this the hard way."

"I told Tre I'm done."

Shivs withdrew his gun. "Seth, my man, wrong answer, bro."

"Go ahead, Shivs. Shoot me and Tre gets nothing. Go ahead." Seth taunted and stepped closer.

"I will shoot you." Shivs brandished the weapon.

A shadowy figure at the rear of the breezeway caught Seth's attention, but instinct told him the man was Holston and not another Kingstonian.

HOLSTON'S ADVANCE mimicking the stealth of a large predatory cat, surprised Seth and he kept the two dumbasses distracted, assisting his protector's approach.

A knife in hand, Holston approached Trigs.

His hand covering Trigs' mouth, Holston jerked the man's head backward, immobilizing Trigs and rendering him speechless. The cold steel blade of his knife pricked Trigs' throat beneath his jaw.

Shivs too focused on Seth, Trigs was left to fend for himself.

"No noise. No nothing or you're dead before you hit the pavement." Holston spoke into Trigs' ear and dragged him behind the building. He coldcocked Trigs and secured his hands and feet.

Holston retraced his steps and pressed the barrel of his Glock 40 into the base of Shivs' skull.

"Nice and slow, lower the gun. Do something stupid scumbag and your brain matter decorates the walls."

Shivs obeyed and Holston issued another command.

"Place your other hand on your back. Seth, take the gun and go," Holston said.

The weapon in Seth's hands, and his client out of harm's way, Holston spoke a third time.

"Slowly. No sudden movements, friend."

"I ain't your friend. You'll pay for this." The crack in Shivs' voice belied his bravado.

"I advise staying quiet too. One peep, and you meet your maker. Now move."

Holston escorted Shivs from the breezeway. No one, other than Seth, aware of the volatile confrontation.

SETH RESISTED RUSHING into Logan's room and peering out the window. Instead of satisfying his curiosity, he poured himself a glass of iced water and sank onto the couch. He lost track of the time until a text pinged on his phone.

He rose and admitted Holston.

"There's nothing you need to know." Holston retrieved the gun from the breakfast bar.

"Wasn't going to ask, but do you want something to drink?"

"Sure. Thanks."

"I'm assuming those two won't be bothering me anymore."

Holston stayed tight-lipped.

Seth filled another glass with ice and water and handed it to Holston.

Holston propped himself against the living room wall and Seth returned to the sofa.

Neither speaking, Seth broke the peace. "Tre will be furious."

"Yup." Holston sipped his water.

"How did you know?"

"It's what I'm paid to do."

"True."

"Seth, my job is making sure nothing happens to you. Everything I do ensures your safety. Is Natalie working tonight?"

"Nice change of subject. Yeah, she is, but off the next two days."
Seth smiled.

"When can you play again?" Holston finished his drink.

"Next week. Two more practices wearing the non-contact jersey
and if the doctor clears me, I can resume regular practices and scrim-
mages. Your wife must be upset you're down here babysitting me."

"Nice change of subject." Holston grinned.

His charge staring at the window prompted Holston placing a hand
on his shoulder. "Seth, *we* will protect you."

"Tre's not just going back to Chicago because he lost two bangers.
He'll send more."

"Seth, the DEA can use your inside information on the
Kingstonians."

"That's a sure way to guarantee I'm pushing up daisies sooner
rather than later."

"Not with the right precautions and my protection," Holston said.

"What? Witness protection? Yeah, right, and there goes my
chance at—"

"No, I can protect you."

Seth's silence prompted Holston's next remark.

"You need to trust me. I have the resources to protect you. It's the
only way you'll break free of them."

Again, Seth stayed silent, Holston's words sinking in, he asked,
"Marshall is on board with this?"

"Marshall is the reason I'm here."

Seth's brows arched, and Holston grinned. "I'll share what's necessary, nothing more. I work with the Boston PD but it's a cover. I'm a
former Army Ranger trained in Black Ops, and I served with the
European Anti-Terrorist Task Force unit. We'll leave it at that."

Seth nodded. "Got it."

"I'll keep you alive, Seth. That's a promise." Holston checked his
watch. "I'm heading out. Stay put. I'll text once I'm back."

"Dare I ask where you're going?" Seth chuckled and rose from the
couch.

Holston paused at the door. "I'm hungry."

"Uh-huh."

Seth locked the door behind Holston and sank onto the couch. Stretched out, he turned on the TV, found an interesting channel, and texted Natalie.

The two texted until Natalie's dispatcher assigned her a call. Exhaustion settling in, Seth dozed off.

The deadbolt and lock turning on the door snapped Seth awake.

"Hey, Seth." Kimmie entered the apartment, carrying several bags.

"Hey." Seth darted to his feet and relieved her of the groceries, placing them on the counter. "Are there more?"

"Nope. Have you eaten?"

"No."

"How do tacos sound?"

"Fine. Kimmie, you are being careful, right?"

"Seth. Stop worrying about me. And yes, I am." Kimmie patted his arm.

"I can stay at Natalie's until this is over. Logan will kill me if anything happens to you."

"Seth, with Logan away, I feel better having you here."

"You sure? What if something happens because of me?"

Kimmie rummaged around in her purse and withdrew a handgun. "This is always with me. And, yeah, I can shoot, without missing."

"Okay, that's good to know. Kimmie, be honest with me. Should I buy a gun? I mean, I can shoot, but…forget it. My past will prevent me from having one." Seth leaned against the counter.

"Seth, stop doubting yourself. I believe people can change if they want to. Look, it's obvious something terrible happened in your past, but you have the chance at a dream thousands of kids can only fantasize about."

"Everyone keeps telling me that.'

"Because it's true. My brother plays in the NHL, and I've been around the sport my entire life. You're good. Really good. NHL good, Seth. I hope Logan makes it too, but you will." Kimmie bumped his shoulder.

"Thanks, Kimmie. Until Marshall, no one has believed in me." Seth offered a half-smile.

"I'm not prying but how did you meet Marshall? Most players who are offered tryouts or sign contracts played in college, junior hockey, or on other pro teams."

"Let's start dinner and I'll tell you. You have the right to know. My past may affect you, Logan, and the entire team.

CURLED ON THE COUCH, a throw pillow clutched in her lap, Kimmie stared across the coffee table at Seth.

"Seth, I'm sorry."

"It's okay. No one can change it. It happened." Seth shrugged.

"I appreciate you confiding in me. I promise everything you said stays between us."

"Logan already knows. He's my roommate, so he needed to. I assumed he'd told you."

"Nope, he didn't. If Logan promises something, he keeps it."

"Uh, this is a two-way street. I'm always here to listen too. It's nice having…friends. Real friends."

"The one thing you'll learn quick with hockey, is we're family, Seth. Speaking of hockey, it's game time."

"Popcorn?" Seth rose from the chair.

"And nachos." Kimmie smiled and followed Seth to the kitchen.

Their snacks fixed, the pair made themselves comfortable in the living room and settled in to watch the game.

CHAPTER 16

atalie signed off and drove to Seth's apartment complex. She parked the patrol car, released Elvis from the rear, and scrutinized the parking lot on her walk across it. At the bottom of the staircase she paused, checking the area again, and climbed the stairs to the second floor.

She unlocked the door and Elvis raced straight to Seth's room.

"Elvis." The dog ignored her command. "Damn it, dog." She hurried after him, but Elvis arrived first.

Her dog standing on top of Seth licking his face brought a smile and she leaned against the closed door observing them.

"Elvis, heel."

The dog jumped off Seth and stretched out alongside him. His dark brown eyes staring at Seth.

"Morning." Natalie's sexy posture ignited Seth's libido, but Elvis' whining demanded immediate attention. Seth pointed at Natalie. "Stay right there."

Seth rolled the dog onto his back and scratching his tummy he buried his face into the side of Elvis' head and spoke.

The canine flipped onto his feet and leapt off the bed.

Seth rose and padded across the room to Natalie and kissed her.

"Need help undressing, officer?" He nuzzled her neck.

"Hmm, depends on why." Natalie tilted her head, exposing her throat to Seth's exploration.

"Sorry, Nat but the gear is in the way." Seth's hand loosened her hair from its ponytail. "I have to have you, now."

"Love me, Seth." Natalie removed her gun belt and lowered it to the floor.

Seth unbuttoned her uniform shirt and freed her of it and her bullet proof vest. The rest of her clothing followed, and he cupped her breasts, coaxing her nipples into hardened peaks.

He bent his knees, lowering his mouth to her abdomen and his tongue trailed a path downward.

"Fucking shit, Seth, love me." Natalie arched against the door.

"Not yet." He nudged her legs apart. "Mouth or fingers?"

"Seth." Natalie's chest heaved.

"Tell me." Now on his knees, Seth licked along the edge of her panties, dipping a finger beneath them, he teased her core.

"Seth, please."

"Tell me." He pulled his finger away.

"Mouth. Hell, whatever. I need something, Seth. Now, please." Natalie wiggled against the door, pushing her hips further away from it.

"So, needy." Seth, using his teeth, ripped her underwear off.

His hands on her thighs, he maneuvered his six-foot-three frame between her legs. Seth's tongue wrought havoc on Natalie, and she moaned her pleasure.

Her fingers gripping his shoulders, she dug her fingernails into his skin.

Natalie's orgasm burst upon her fast and intense and she slithered down the door.

Seth pulled her flat on the floor, crawled between her legs, lifted her ankles onto his shoulders and plundered her sweetness.

Natalie writhing in the ecstasy of a second climax, he retrieved a condom from the nightstand. He gathered her against him and pulled her onto his hardened shaft.

She clung to him, meeting his thrusts. "Oh, my God, Seth. More."

Aware of others in the apartment, Natalie burrowed into his neck, muffling her scream.

Seth increased his tempo, but his release hovered out of reach, and he lowered Natalie onto her back. Their eyes on each other, he spoke.

"Nat, I want, need you so bad. I'm afraid I'll lose control, but by God, I—"

"Love me, Seth. Love all of me."

"If it gets too rough, I'll hurt you."

"No, you won't."

"Yes, I will. You're my high, Nat."

"Let me up. Sit against the bed." Natalie pushed him from her.

Seth obeyed.

Natalie climbed onto Seth. "I'll do you the other way afterward."

"No, not until the test comes back."

"I can do it without—"

"No. Now for God's sake, Natalie, fuck the shit out of me." Seth's hands spanned her waist, and he pulled her down, and thrust into her.

Natalie heeded Seth's wishes and set a savage rhythm, their bodies slapping against each other.

Seth's pleasurable moans increasing, Natalie sucked on the tender flesh of his throat. Aware he didn't mind rough sex, she peppered bite marks along his collarbone.

Natalie arched her neck and ground her hips, and taking Seth to the edge, she catapulted him toward an explosive euphoria.

Seth clutched Natalie's waist and he pinned her hips against him, stilling her movement. His climax erupted and he rammed into her, crying out his pleasure.

His hands dropping from her waist, Natalie slumped against Seth's sweat soaked chest.

Their labored breathing easing, Seth's eyelids cracked open. He swiped aside a wet strand of her hair and cupped her chin, lifting her head from his chest.

Her lids fluttering open, he smiled and captured her mouth, his kiss gentle, he spoke against her lips. "I love you, Natalie. I love you more than life itself."

Natalie trailed a finger along his stubbled jaw. "I love you too, Seth."

"It's not just the sex for me, Nat."

"Seth, baby. It's not for me either. Although, I will say I enjoy the added benefit."

He caught the mischievous twinkle in her eyes and chuckled.

"Yeah, me too. Are you okay? I always worry it's too rough. Nat, I'd kill myself if I hurt you." A hint of fear laced his tone.

"Baby, trust me, I'll tell you if it is. It's passion, baby. Passion between two people who love and crave each other."

"Is it?"

Natalie straightened into a sitting position.

"Seth, answer me honestly, okay?"

He nodded.

"When you serviced your clients, did you just wham bam, do them and be done with it?"

"Yeah."

"Did you care if they enjoyed it?"

"I did whatever they told me to do. Why?"

Natalie studied his puzzled expression and a pang of hurt stabbed her stomach.

"You never experienced pleasure did you."

"It wasn't my place to. My job was pleasuring them. Can we change subjects?"

"I'm sorry. One more question, please."

"Okay."

"Did you come with any of them?"

Seth answered right out. "No."

"That's the difference, baby. There's passion between us. Neither of us will hurt the other because we have passion. Our pleasure intensifies from ensuring the other reaches theirs." Natalie caressed his cheek. Her finger traced the fresh scar running into his eyebrow.

"It scares me that it gets crazy and wild."

"Seth, baby, trust me, I'm more than capable of stopping you. Okay, now I'm exhausted. Either let me sleep or make love to me again."

A wicked grin replaced Seth's serious expression and he carried Natalie to the bed. He left her for the time needed to dispose of the condom and retrieve a new one.

Seth lowered himself next to her. His mouth hovering above hers, his breath grazed her lips.

"I'm making slow, sensual love to you, Nat."

"No, you're not." She locked one hand behind his head and reaching between their bodies, grasped his shaft and guided his engorged flesh into her heat.

Seth plunged into her. He withheld loving her and enjoyed the sensations of her tight sheath molding around him.

"God, you drive me crazy. You're hot. So, hot, Nat."

"Quench your desire, Seth." Natalie's lips quivering from with-holding her laughter at his expression, she shook her head. "I like historical romances."

"Okay."

Seth controlled his baser urges and fulfilled his promise. She begged for release, but he maintained his pace, and clutched her hips, holding her butt off the bed.

He pumped, firm and slow. Each one bringing a deeper moan from Natalie. His hold kept her from writhing and her begging increased.

"Now, Seth! Now!"

He shifted one hand and stroked her pearl with each new thrust.

"Oh, dear God, that's...Seth."

Natalie's world spun out of control and unconsciousness threatened her from the intensity of the looming ecstasy. Seth pulled out of her, and using his tongue and fingers, he tipped her into delirium. She grabbed a pillow and screamed into it, her body convulsing from the most powerful orgasm of her life.

SETH EASED out of the bed at nine. He dressed and gestured to Elvis, and the dog followed him from the room. He clipped the dog's leash on and the two left the apartment.

One foot on the stairs, Seth's cellphone pinged an incoming text. He stopped and read it, Elvis staring at him, tongue hanging out of his mouth. Seth tucked the phone back into his pocket and tugged on Elvis' leash, and the pair met Holston at the edge of the sidewalk.

"Natalie, awake?"

"No."

"Kirk's meeting us at the arena for your practice and you'll give your statement to him afterward." Holston scratched Elvis' head.

"Okay." Seth nodded.

"Seth. I promise, I'm keeping you safe."

"I know. Look, I've always taken care of myself. People caring about my welfare is a foreign concept for me."

"No explanation is needed, but you best become accustomed to it. You're good. Really good, and from my dealings with Marshall, he went out on a limb for you because he sees your potential. Trust him, Seth. I know it's hard but forget the past. Put it behind you. Move on, it's time." Holston smiled and patted Seth's arm.

"Are you coming up?"

"Nah, five's a crowd." Holston smiled.

"Any more than two's a crowd." Seth grinned, Elvis completed his business, and the two returned to the apartment.

LATER IN THE DAY, Natalie, Holston, and Kirk, the DEA agent they were working with, entered the arena and sat on the top row of the section behind the team's bench during their practice.

On the ice, Seth stopped at the bench, and raised his stick in their direction.

Natalie waved, but once he resumed skating, she addressed Kirk, but kept her eyes on Seth. "I know the answer, but if there is any way to avoid having Seth testify, it would be preferred. We're anticipating Tremaine, or his thugs to come after him."

"I'll need confirmation with the Chicago office, but if his information proves fruitful with busts, I'm sure someone will roll. We'll have to verify the information he gives us," Kirk said.

"There'll be tons of speculation on its validity." Natalie's gaze stayed on Seth.

"True. We both know how most jurors view gangsters and drug dealers," Kirk said, and spotting the two men, in black suits, sitting in the adjacent section, he tilted his head in their direction. "What's with the two goons and Ice Bitch?"

"Oh, them. Aleksander Miszczak's bodyguards and his girlfriend. His father is a high-profile scientist in Poland, and his mother is a linguistics professor."

"Russians, not Polish," Holston supplied.

"Interesting." Kirk studied the group.

"That's an understatement. Ice Bitch. I like that." Natalie chuckled. "She's a piece of work too. There's something about her I don't trust. She's super possessive and jealous beyond shit over Alek."

No longer interested in Aleksander's bodyguards or Natasha Kuznetsova, Natalie twisted in her seat, and added, "Back to our situation. He's agreeing to provide a verbal and written statement, but only if given a written guarantee of immunity against all charges."

Holston listened but he continued observing the two Russians, and Alek's girlfriend.

"It's right here. Unfortunately, I can't promise he won't have to testify, Nat." Kirk tapped the manila folder. "You want to look it over?"

"Read through legal mumble jumble and miss my guy skating, no thanks. I trust you. I know where to find you." Natalie winked at Kirk.

THE PRACTICE FINISHED and the players exiting the ice, Holston excused himself and wove his way through the stands and to the tunnel. Natalie and Kirk rose and headed to the meeting room.

Upon entering, Natalie and Kirk greeted Cooper. The two men

having met a week prior to discuss the various possible implications from Seth speaking out against the Kingstonians.

Kirk and Cooper talking, Natalie spotted a pair of older gentlemen in the room.

"Natalie Savage, Agent Kirk Darby. Patrick Hawks, Boston's owner and Lou Gwyn, Boston's general manager. Their involvement is essential. They have a vested monetary interest in Seth," Cooper said.

The group exchanged handshakes and settled in around the table.

Cooper's assistant delivered pitchers of water and glasses, and Kirk answered Lou and Patrick's questions and reassured them every precaution was being taken to ensure Seth's safety.

CHAPTER 17

Seth raked his fingers through his hair and paced Marshall's office.

"Ready?"

Marshall's question compounded Seth's nerves.

"Yeah, Coach." Seth fiddled with his shirt collar.

"Oh, here." Marshall handed Seth an envelope.

Seth hesitating, Marshall snatched it back, tearing it open. His lips pursed but he cracked a smile. "You're good."

A smile surfacing, Seth accepted the sheet of paper, folded it, and slipped it into his jacket pocket.

"Time to go." Marshall opened the door, nodding at Holston waiting in the corridor and the three walked in silence to the elevator.

Seth's pace slowed the closer he came to the meeting room.

Marshall grasping his arm, halted him.

He eyed Marshall and inhaled a deep, lung-filling breath.

"Seth, you can back out," Marshall said.

"No, Coach. I need to put my past behind me. I'm not living the rest of my life looking over my shoulder."

"Ok but remember this. You're not alone. We're here to support you and will protect you."

"Let's do this." Seth smiled and entered the meeting room.

He recognized Kirk and Cooper, but the two older gentlemen were unfamiliar. Cooper introduced Patrick Hawks and Lou Gwyn, and Seth shook their hands, and thanked them for the opportunity to achieve his dream.

Seth selected a seat between Marshall and Natalie and entwined his fingers with hers. A brief smile followed.

Seated opposite Seth, Kirk spoke, "Seth, with your consent I'll record this meeting. Normally, I don't record interviews, but in this case, I believe it's necessary. This…" He pointed at an official sheet of paper on top of the folder in front of him. "…is a written guarantee of immunity against prosecution for any crimes you've committed and disclose here. The immunity is provided on the basis you are truthful to the best of your knowledge, forthcoming, and fully cooperate with this investigation and any subsequent inquires related to the information you divulge today."

The paper and a pen handed to Seth, quiet enveloped the room. He signed it and slid it back to Kirk.

"Seth, before you start, are you sure you want all of us listening?" Patrick Hawks asked.

"Yes, sir. You have a vested interest in me. You've given me a chance at my dream. I've nothing to hide."

Seth met each person's eyes, lingering longest on Natalie's and then ended on Kirk's.

"Whenever you're ready, Seth." Kirk nodded.

"Sure." Seth glanced at Natalie.

"There's no rush. You can do this but stop if you need a break. I love you and I'm right here." Natalie squeezed his hand.

"Mr. Hawks. Mr. Gwyn. I'm not sure how much of my past you're already privy to, but I hope you understand everything I did was to survive…and feed my habit."

"Seth, we understand." Patrick Hawks included his colleague in his gesture." "We spoke with Marshall prior to offering you a contract. We're aware of your criminal record and former drug habit."

Seth inhaled and spoke, "I have no idea who my parents are. I've no idea if they're dead, alive, or if I have siblings. I was eight or nine when I ran away from the last foster home. I never stayed in one more than six months, other than the last one…where the abuse started a few hours after I arrived."

"Do you remember the family's name?" Marshall asked.

"No, but there were never any girls, only boys." Seth paused, memories swarming his brain, "I remember the address, and everything about the house."

Natalie stifled a curse.

"I thought the streets would be safer." Seth sipped on the glass of water. Natalie's thumb rubbed across his other hand.

"I was hungry, and no one let me work to earn money. Everyone said I was too young, so I shoplifted food, and pilfered clothes out of the dumpsters when I couldn't steal any. I slept wherever I found a dry place. I lasted a year on my own, then I met Tremaine Kingston. More like he found me. Winter was coming. He offered me food, shelter, and money if I worked for him. I figured what the hell, and I ran drugs for him, I figured I'd make enough money and leave Chicago."

Seth shared the details of his duties for the Kingstonians.

A hush consumed the room once he finished speaking.

"Let's take a break," Kirk suggested.

Seth gulped the rest of his water and rose.

"Agent Darby, can I step out?"

"Sure." Kirk smiled his assent.

Natalie followed Seth into the hallway. "Are you okay?" Her hands clutched his.

"Yeah, that was harder than I thought." Seth braced himself against the wall.

"Seth, I'm proud of you. You can still change your mind."

"No, this is for the next kid Tremaine turns into a prostituting junkie. I dreamed of escaping that life, but that hope faded every day, and I was ready to give up…then I met Marshall. Now I have a chance at something I've always dreamed about but wasn't possible, and for the first time, I care what people think." Seth's eyes redirected away from Natalie's.

"I'm proud of you, baby. It takes a super strong person to do what you're doing and talking is the first step to healing and moving forward." Natalie stretched on tiptoes and kissed his cheek.

"Those guys in there, Hawks and Gwyn, they're rich, Nat. Millions, billions, rich. I'm a recovering addict and former prostitute. Once they hear that, they'll release me, Then what, Nat? I have no skills, other than some stuff I learned at the auto body shop? I *refuse* going back to a life of drugs and prostitution."

"Have faith, Seth. My guess, and this is the cop in me and my years of experience speaking, they're already aware of everything. Those guys prospered from researching every investment they have and ever will make, including you."

"I guess you're right. Still, it's…"

"Embarrassing?" Natalie tilted her head.

"Yeah. Telling you and Marshall is different. I trust you two. I don't know them."

"Seth, trust them. Your future is in their hands. Come on, baby. Let's finish this up." Natalie entwined their fingers and the two returned to the meeting room.

SETH HAVING REVEALED the sordid details of his time with the Kingstonians, silence encompassed the room.

Kirk broke it. "Seth, I'm personally meeting with our agents in Chicago tomorrow. They may request to speak with you directly. I wish this was all we needed from you."

"I understand." Seth inhaled and added, "Agent Darby, I'll testify against Tremaine or any of the others, if necessary."

Kirk nodded. "Good. Thank you. If no one has any questions, I'll take my leave. Mr. Hawks, Mr. Gwyn, thank you."

"You're welcome, Agent Darby. The quicker this information is delivered, the sooner action can be taken, and Seth can relax," Patrick Hawks said, his gaze taking in everyone at the table. "My private jet is at Agent Darby's disposal, and for any necessary travel for Seth."

Kirk said his goodbyes and left.

Patrick spoke, "I took the liberty of making reservations for dinner." His smile widening, he gestured at the door.

The group rose and headed out.

Seth approached Patrick. "Sir. Thank you for taking a risk on me, you won't regret it. I promise, I won't disappoint you, sir."

"Son, you're welcome. I am sorry you went through that, but you overcame a horrendous situation and you're an inspiration to others. You'll be a good fit with our organization. Listen to Marshall. Now let us enjoy a hearty dinner and discuss pleasanter subjects. I'm starving." Patrick smiled and patted Seth's shoulder.

"Thank you, sir." Seth extended his hand. Patrick shook it and the two walked out of the room together.

"Baby, everything okay?" Natalie cocked her head.

"Yeah, I wanted to thank Mr. Hawks and promise I wouldn't disappoint him." Seth smiled. "Oh, and here." He handed her a piece of paper.

Natalie read it, smiled, and hugged Seth. "Great news, baby. and you won't disappoint anyone." Natalie looped her arms around his neck and kissed him.

"Come on you two, dinner is waiting." Patrick Hawks chuckled, interrupting their interlude.

"We better go." Natalie tangled her fingers with Seth's, and they left.

SETH, shirtless and alone in the apartment, combed his fingers through his damp hair, turned on the television, and entered the kitchen for a glass of juice.

Poised to pour the beverage, the voice blaring from the TV caught his attention. Each day, for the past week and a half, he tuned into the news, anticipating word of the Kingstonians' and Tremaine's arrest. Natalie having informed him that it would take time for the DEA and other authorities to gather intelligence and conduct their raids.

"Today, in the early-morning hours, agents from the DEA, ATF, and Chicago police initiated a massive operation against the city's most feared and powerful gang, the Kingstonians. The various raids resulted in dozens of arrests, along with the seizure of an undisclosed quantity of drugs, weapons, and money. A spokesman for the DEA, who coordinated the operation, verified the arrest of high-ranking members of the gang, but the organization's leader, Tremaine Kingston, escaped capture. We will be…"

Seth dashed to his bedroom and shrugged into a shirt. He grabbed his keys and cellphone and left the apartment.

Holston shoved away from the wall. "Seth."

Seth ignored him and bolted to his SUV, cranked the engine, engaged the vehicle's hands-free Bluetooth system, and reversed out of his parking spot.

Natalie's voice mail greeting him, he left a message.

The broadcaster's words echoing through Seth's brain, he maneuvered through the traffic at a frantic rate. His driving erratic, he steered the SUV onto the highway and rocketed past a Charleston County Sheriff's car.

Blue lights flashing in Seth's mirrors, the patrol car closed the distance between them. Seth peeked at his speedometer and moved into the right-hand lane. The police vehicle followed.

He slammed his hand against the steering wheel and eased his foot from the gas pedal. The Cayenne slowing, he maneuvered the vehicle out of traffic. A call ringing through the hands-free system, he placed the car in park, and hit the answer button.

"Seth, baby. What's wrong?"

His words rushed, he answered, "Nat, Tremaine escaped and I'm getting pulled over."

"Woo, slow down. Tremaine—"

"Nat. The cop's approaching."

Seth opened his window.

"Cop? Seth—"

"Sir. I need your license, registration, and proof of insurance. Do you know why—"

"Seth."

"Sir, please end the call."

"Like hell he's ending the call. This is Officer—" Natalie's strident tones rang through the Cayenne's speakers.

"Nat. It's fine. I'll call you back." Seth hit the end button and disconnected the call. "I'm sorry, sir. My girlfriend is a police officer. I called her before I left my apartment, but she didn't answer. She just called back."

Holston's black Tahoe, joining them on the side of the road, appeared in Seth's side mirror, catching his brief attention. The deputy also noted the arrival of the SUV.

"That's my bodyguard, Holston Karz, sir."

The deputy eyeing the Tahoe and on the verge of speaking an incoming call rang through the Cayenne's interior.

"That's Natalie calling back. Can I answer?"

"No."

Seth hit the end call button.

"She'll keep calling. I'm sorry I was speeding. I—"

The ringing sounded again.

"Go ahead answer it." The deputy, shaking his head, gestured at the phone.

"Hey, Nat."

A barrage of questions and commands erupted.

"Nat. I'm okay. Holston's parked behind the cop. Tre got away and I panicked."

"Fucking, shit. Does Holston know?"

"I don't know."

"Seth, give your phone to the officer. I can't hear you through the traffic."

He complied and the deputy stepped away from the Cayenne.

The call ended, and the deputy returned Seth's phone.

"I'm sorry, Officer. I panicked."

"I'm only writing you a warning. Thank Natalie later."

"Thank you." Seth produced the requested documents, and the deputy returned to his patrol car.

The deputy handing Seth his documents and ticket, said, "Slow it down, Doyle."

"Yes, sir, and I am sorry."

Seth eased the Cayenne into traffic and maintaining the speed limit, resumed his journey, Holston on his tail.

His Cayenne parked, Seth exited, and waited for Holston. His bodyguard stormed across the lot and Seth braced himself for the onslaught.

"Pull another stunt like that, and I'll kick your ass. Got it?" Holston jabbed Seth in the chest.

"Yes, sir." The two crossing the parking lot, Seth added, "I'm sorry. I panicked. How the hell did he get away? They promised."

Holston opened the players' entrance door, ushered Seth inside, and said, "Seth, we'll find him, but you keep your head straight, okay? You didn't survive all those years on the streets because of luck. You understand what I'm saying?"

"Yeah."

Seth and Holston walked into Marshall's office without knocking.

"Coach, they talked about the raids on the news. They said Tre got away."

"I heard."

"And you didn't call me?" Seth paced inside the office. Holston occupied the doorway, his shoulder braced against the doorframe, blocking it.

Marshall nor Holston, blind to the severity of the situation, Seth's pacing an added indication the young defenseman was rattled, and fearful.

"Seth."

"He's coming for me, Coach. He'll know it was me. You have no clue what he does to people who betray him. It's a very slow and painful death."

"He needs to get past me first," Holston said, maintaining his calm, casual posture.

"You can't be with me twenty-four seven." Seth eyed Holston.

"I can and I will."

"You going to watch me shit and piss?"

"If I have to." Holston's eyes met Seth's.

"Fucking great. So, now I have no privacy for anything." Seth slammed his fist into the wall.

"Seth, let's skate." Marshall rose from his chair and circled around his desk.

"Why?"

"Because, I said so." His hand on Seth's shoulder, Marshall urged him out of the office. Holston stepped aside and followed them.

"Outside of this arena, even if he's with Natalie, he's never out of your sight." Marshall commanded Holston.

"No problem."

On the ice, Marshall diverted Seth's focus away from Tremaine and spent the next two hours working with his young protégé.

The two standing by the boards near the bench, they squirted water into their mouths.

"Coach, I'm sorry I freaked. Tremaine *will* find me. And…" He paused, sucking down more water. "He has videos of me…you know."

"The possibility of their release concerns you?" Marshall leaned his elbow on top of the boards.

"Nah, nothing I can do. It happened. Why deny it. But I'd prefer if the entire world doesn't see them." Seth gulped more water and added. "Coach, I'll lose in a fight against Tre. The one time I fought him, he kicked my ass."

"Seth, you're stronger, more physically fit, and losing only happens if you let those doubts rule you up here." Marshall pointed at his head.

"I guess. I mean, I can defend myself, but when it comes to Tremaine…"

"That's here." Marshall tapping Seth's head, reiterated his point.

"I suppose you're right."

Neither was aware fate planned to test Marshall's words sooner than either anticipated.

CHAPTER 18

F ive days later, without any incidents, Seth relaxed his guard. Holston upheld his promise and became Seth's permanent shadow whenever he ventured outside his or Natalie's apartment. Inside the arena, he kept his distance, but lurked nearby.

DRESSED IN COMPRESSION SHORTS, a team hockey t-shirt, Seth entered the equipment room, skates in hand. He finished sharpening one blade and placed the skate on the counter. His pre-game music blaring in his ears, he worked on the second skate.

Seth's back to the door, he concentrated on his task. One slip and he risked sawing off a finger or inflicting a severe cut.

The music mixed with the grinding metal drowned out Tremaine's approach. Between Seth's instinct, and pure luck, he avoided the knife blade aiming at the center of his back. He swung his skate, and the razor-sharp edge sliced Tremaine's bicep.

Seth raised his arm, blocking another strike, but Tremaine's blade ripped across his forearm. Anger and adrenaline propelled his attacker's frantic swings, and the tip of the weapon dragged across Seth's abdomen. His compression shirt preventing a deeper cut.

Backstepping, Seth avoided a direct stab. The movement propelled him into the counter holding the skate sharpener. Tremaine swung the knife a second time and Seth grabbed his assailant's arm, the knife an inch from his neck.

His teeth clenched and grunting, he tightened his hold on Tremaine's wrist, forcing it against the skate sharpener. He slammed it against the machine but failed dislodging the weapon.

Tremaine's knee rammed into Seth's groin. Pain speared through his body, and he lost the advantage. The knife streaking toward Seth, he dodged, and the blade missed its mark, but scored his chest and raked his shoulder.

A second and direct blow in the groin winded Seth, and he stumbled. His cheek hit the corner of the bench, leaving a deep gouge near his left eye. Stars and a wave of darkness blinded him, hindering his fighting ability.

Tremaine's fury-charged aggression countered Seth's physical strength, and his survivalist instinct kept him from suffering serious harm.

Desperation fueled Tremaine's onslaught and his knife aimed for Seth's throat. The cool edge of steel sliced a path from his collarbone to his neck.

NATALIE, and Elvis on his lead, entered the arena through the players' entrance. The duo reaching the hallway connecting the various team rooms, Elvis' abrupt lunge yanked the leash from Natalie's hand.

Elvis wove through the swarm of people in the hallway heading in the same direction. Natalie struggled keeping him in view. His continuous barking mixed with the clamor of a brawl.

"Get the police down here," someone ordered, and Natalie rushed forward, pushing people aside.

"In the equipment room." An arena worker pointed.

Natalie glimpsed Holston darting into the room. Elvis shot across the threshold at the same time.

The flash of metal from Holston's handgun pitched ice down Natalie's spine. Her chest pinched, and she drew her weapon.

Natalie burst into the room and into a scene of chaos. Elvis' vicious growls drowned out the sounds from two men grappling on the floor.

Her partner, spotting an opportunity to join the fight, became a blur of flying fur, and knocked Tremaine off Seth. His powerful jaws clamped onto the man's wrist. Steel glinted, and the dog yelped but held fast.

Holston trained the barrel of his gun on Seth's assailant. "Move and you leave in a body bag."

Both aiming their weapons at the man trapped beneath a furious Elvis, Natalie demanded the man drop his weapon.

"Get him the fuck off me."

"Drop the knife and I'll call him off." Natalie clenched her jaw, calmed her breathing, and focused on Tremaine Kingston.

"Get him off. Fucking dog. I'll kill all of you." Tremaine shoved at Elvis, and the dog's teeth dug deeper.

"Drop the knife!" Holston's command reverberated around the room, and he stepped closer until his target stared down the gun barrel.

"Drop the fucking knife now and I'll call off the dog." Out of the corner of her eye, Natalie observed Seth levering himself to a sitting position.

"Fucking dog, get him off." Despite Tremaine's strenuous efforts, he failed dislodging Elvis.

Holston stomped on Tremaine's ankle and him and Natalie spat additional commands at Tremaine.

Elvis' hold on the gangster unrelenting.

"Drop the fucking knife. Now!" Holston repeated the warning, his tone demanding immediate obedience.

Tremaine complied.

The knife clattering to the floor, Holston kicked it aside.

Natalie commanded, "Elvis, heel. Heel! Stay."

Elvis released his grip and sat but kept watch on Tremaine.

Her eyes trained on Tremaine, she squatted, and retrieved Elvis' leash and handed it to Holston. She holstered her weapon and withdrew her handcuffs.

"Seth, are you okay?" Holston's focus stayed on Natalie cuffing Tremaine.

"Yeah."

"We need paramedics, and bring towels," Holston directed those staying safely outside the door, but his eyes never wavered from Tremaine.

Restrained and yanked off the floor, Tremaine glared at Seth, and pulled against Natalie's hold.

"This ain't over Seth. I swear I'll kill you. You're dead. Dead."

Tremaine's belligerence prompted Elvis barring his teeth and lunging forward.

"Elvis, heel!" Natalie's sharp directive prevented Elvis from latching onto the gangster a second time.

The dog sat and Holston dropped his leash.

"Let's go, scumbag." Holston jerked Tremaine away from Natalie and escorted him out of the room.

"Fucking dog, I'll kill him, too. I'll kill every one of you. You too, bitch, once I bang—"

"Get that piece of trash out of my arena." Marshall's voice boomed through the hallway and his deadly gaze met Tremaine's.

"He's a fucking, cocksucking junkie. I'll kill you too." Tremaine vowed.

"Yeah, scumbag." Without flinching, Marshall stepped closer, his chest inches away from Tremaine's. The two stared at each other until Holston dragged Tremaine away.

"You'll be back on the streets begging for a hit, Seth, and sucking more cocks. Fucker. I'll kill you. Everyone will know you're a male-whoring junkie…" Tremaine's continuous threats and derogatory remarks echoed off the concrete walls.

Tremaine gone, the tension within the room and hallway diminished, and havoc calmed.

. . .

NATALIE, squatting at Seth's side, accepted a towel Ansley tossed her way.

Ansley, positioned on the other side of Seth, wasted no time examining his wounds.

Seth stroked Elvis. His fingers encountering a stickiness on the dog's fur, he pulled Elvis onto his lap.

"Hey, boy. You hurt?"

Elvis stretched out and Seth inspected him further, finding a wound on the dog's front left leg.

"Nat."

Natalie noting Seth's wounds, raised a brow.

"Elvis. He's bleeding."

"Uh, so are you," Natalie said, scrutinizing his wounds.

"Seth, let go of Elvis, please." Ansley's hand rested on Seth's arm.

"He's hurt. He's bleeding." Seth speared his fingers into the dog's ruff. "He saved my life."

"Yeah, well, you're bleeding, too." Ansley ran her hands along the dog. "It's not life threatening. He'll be fine. Can you stand?"

"Yeah."

Natalie lifted Elvis off Seth's lap and handed her dog to the assistant trainer, and he left ahead of them. One officer, having stayed behind, helped a paramedic hoist Seth off the floor.

"Adam, scratch Seth," Marshall said.

"Coach. I'm okay. I can play."

"We'll see. It's not a request."

The medic assisting Seth on one side, Ansley on his other, and the rest trailed behind.

Marshall stopped at the training room door and addressed the crowd in the hallway. "Clear out. Let the police do their job, and we have a game."

Inside the room, Elvis sat on one of the exam tables and Seth approached, stroking the dog's head. He cupped the dog's face and kissed Elvis' snout. "Thanks, buddy. I owe you."

Elvis slapped several enthusiastic licks on Seth's face.

"Seth. I need to look you over and he needs attention too. "Ansley said.

He hesitated.

"Seth, please," Natalie said, lavishing attention on the dog.

The assistant trainer caring for Elvis, Natalie joined Seth.

His shirt discarded, per Ansley's request, Natalie studied the knife wounds. "You're going to the hospital."

"Nat, I'm fine." Seth grasped her hand.

Natalie ignored the blood coating Seth's palm, and she entangled their fingers.

"You're a doctor now, Doyle?" Ansley questioned and retrieved a sewing kit.

The paramedic finished cleaning the blood from Seth's wounds, Ansley set to work stitching them, including the one at the corner of his eye.

"Nat, he needs a vet. His wound requires stitches and have them check for ligament damage. It's a deep cut," The assistant trainer said.

"Okay." Natalie returned to Elvis and ruffled her K-9 partner's ears.

"Go. I'm fine. Take care of my hero, Nat." Seth urged.

Natalie and Seth exchanged a brief kiss, and she carried Elvis out of the arena.

Finished suturing Seth's various lacerations, Ansley nodded, and he eased off the table.

SETH HEADED to the locker room, intent on dressing for the game, but Marshall blocked the door, and he swallowed a sigh.

Neither speaking, Marshall studied Seth.

"Coach, I need to suit up."

"It's not you're decision."

"Come on, Coach. I'm fine. Honest." Seth straightened.

"Seth, this isn't the streets."

"I know. It's Thackeray. I'm not afraid of him, Coach."

Marshall exhaled. "No, you're not, but if he even suspects you're injured. It's his job to target you."

"Let him." Seth shrugged.

"You have no fear, do you?"

"There's a lot of stuff I'm afraid of, Coach. Showing weakness has never been a choice for me."

More silence stretched between them.

"Suit up, but if I see any distress. One iota of it, you're out."

"Ok. Thanks, and Coach, I promise I'll say something if I'm not a hundred percent."

"Yeah, right."

The two keeping eye contact, Marshall shook his head and ushered Seth back to the training room.

Ansley applied extra padding to the lacerations and wrapped his upper body with ace bandages.

"You're good to go." Ansley crossed her arms. Once Seth left, she shook her head. "Men."

THE FIRST PERIOD concluded with Seth exhibiting no adverse effects from his wounds. He was the recipient of a few hard hits, adding to Marshall's concern for his battered defenseman's health.

Eight minutes left in the second period and the tone of the game changed. The Patriots, initiating a line change and losing control of the puck near center ice, Seth opted staying in. His decision kept their goalie from facing a three-on-one disadvantage.

Seth's maneuver cut the forward's angle, forcing him out of the play. The other two closing in, he focused on the one controlling the puck and his opponent glanced at his line mate, gauging who had the better shot.

His ruse tricked his opponent into passing the puck. Seth adjusted his position, preventing a shot on goal, forcing another pass, and the shot.

Seth twisted his body, deflecting the one-timer, but the puck hit his right side, striking the knife wound. He dropped to the ice, sliding away from his goalie.

The puck trapped beneath him stopped play. He gritted his teeth and pushed himself onto his hands and knees. Ansley appeared in no time.

Pain ripped into his side each time he inhaled, and he slowed his breathing, resting on his haunches.

An unexpected arm hooked around Seth's elbow on his injured side, and he looked upward. His eyes meeting Thackeray's, his nemesis assisted him to his feet.

"That was fucking stupid."

"Yeah, but it kept you from scoring." Seth mustered a smile.

"Stupid ass move, but gutsy. You'll make it, kid." Thackeray's praise startled Seth and he stared at the man.

"Thanks." Seth grimaced.

Ansley alongside him, Seth left the ice.

CHAPTER 19

T he team having returned to Charleston and now on their Christmas break, Seth finished packing his bag and hoisted it onto his shoulder, ignoring the twinge of pain in his side from the healing laceration.

Kimmie having flown to Florida for their game, her and Logan flew to New Hampshire right afterward. Quiet and loneliness blanketed the apartment and Seth blew out a breath.

In Chicago, enjoying time alone was a rarity. He was too busy pursuing his next hit. His existence centered around sinking into a drug-induced delirium and escaping the reality of his world, not what people thought of him.

He couldn't change his past, but the constant support Marshall and his teammates offered kept chipping away at his guarded defenses.

Seth had genuine friends, a promising career, and the best of his world now, Natalie.

Love in any form wasn't an emotion Seth ever expected to experience, and never at first sight, but once he laid eyes on Natalie, she cast a tight net around his heart.

The memory tugged forth a smile.

. . .

THE APARTMENT LOCKED, Seth dumped his bag in the Cayenne's cargo area, texted Natalie, and seated in his vehicle, he paused, contemplating the changes occurring in his life.

Anxiety seldom gripped Seth, but a new challenge faced him, and one he found unnerving. Once Natalie signed off, they'd head to North Carolina to spend Christmas with her family. Seth set his apprehension aside and drove to her apartment.

He unlocked the front door, freed Elvis from his crate, and walked him. The duo returned and made themselves comfortable on the couch. Elvis' injury ended his working career, and upon his retirement from service, Natalie adopted him.

Elvis laying between his legs, his head rested on Seth's thigh.

He stroked the dog's ears, and tired from the long bus ride home, Seth succumbed to sleep.

NATALIE GLANCED at the clock on the cruiser's dash and rolled her eyes. The evening dragged on, but she avoided complaining. The lack of calls refreshing.

An incoming text pinged.

Home. Heading to your place. A heart emoji preceded *love you,* and she smiled.

She replied with a row of heart emojis and ended with, *love you too, see you soon.*

Three months ago, Moira orchestrated a meeting between Seth and her. From the moment she laid eyes on him he snagged her immediate interest. His patience and gentle coaxing wove a tenuous web during their time at the rink, and his subsequent gentle behavior at dinner an odd contrast to his brash exterior. Their intimate encounter on the ice shattered her inhibitions regarding their age difference.

The sex with Seth superseded any of her previous experiences. His kindness, respect for her, and unselfish devotion stole her heart.

Instead of blaming others for his mistakes, his choices, Seth shouldered the weight of his past. Another attribute Natalie loved.

Mixed feelings plagued Natalie throughout her shift. She loved Seth, and she didn't doubt he reciprocated it, but she feared her news threatened changing everything, and it weighed on her.

She spent her free moments figuring out the best way to deliver the news.

To her relief, a day-shift officer signed on an hour early. She radioed out of service, texted her coworker a thank you, and drove home.

Natalie parked her police cruiser alongside Seth's SUV. She dragged in a deep breath and entered her apartment. Darkness greeted her and she assumed Seth was asleep in the bedroom.

Elvis' head lifted from Seth's leg. Assured no unwanted strangers entered the residence, he chilled.

Seth stirred and Natalie smiled.

"Hey, baby. Congratulations on the win. I know you were happy being back in the lineup." Natalie unstrapped her gun belt on her way through the apartment. Seth following, she smiled. His strong arms wrapped around her waist, and he brushed a kiss to her neck.

"Thanks. Quiet night?" His stubbled jaw nuzzled her cheek.

"Yeah. Seth, we need to talk—"

His abrupt jerking away caught Natalie off guard.

She snagged his arm. "Hey, baby, relax."

"Are you dumping me?"

"Uh, no. Sit."

Seth ignored her request. "I prefer hearing bad news standing up."

Seth's reaction prompted her immediate revelation, dousing her well-laid plans of breaking the news to him.

"A baby on the way is bad news?"

Dead silence.

"Seth?"

"You're pregnant?"

"Yeah. I found out today. Seth, I'm sorry I—"

His mouth captured her words.

Natalie broke the kiss, making eye contact. "You're not mad?"

"No, I'm not mad, but do you—"

This time Natalie interrupted. "Seth, I'm keeping the baby, but your career is just starting out and a family is the last thing you need right now. So, I under—"

Seth's finger pressing her lips quieted her. A new spark glittered in his gorgeous blue eyes, scattering the butterflies in her stomach into a frenzy.

"Nat, I love you. It's crazy, but I fell in love with you in the hallway the first day we met. I wanted to ask you to marry me weeks ago, but I figured..."

"I love you, too, baby, and everything has happened quickly, but it's right. I know it here." Natalie tapped the center of her chest. "A lot has changed, but that's life, and we'll be okay if we communicate and trust each other."

"What happens if—"

"When." Natalie smiled.

"When I move up. I want you and the baby with me."

"We'll figure it out. Baby or no baby, you're advancing to the AHL, and the NHL will happen. We have a few hours during the drive to discuss our future. I've already spoken with my shift leader, and it's my decision on how long I work the road, but you have a say in it too."

"You'll have to leave your job when we move, and you love police work, Nat. I'm sorry. I should've been more careful."

"Seth, it takes two to tango, and we tangoed. A lot." A devilish grin creased her face. One hand cupped his groin and a finger on her other hand traced his lips. "I'm not married to my career. Yes, I love it but *you*, and now *our* baby are the two most important things in my life."

Natalie's reply struck a chord deep inside Seth's soul. For the first time in his life, he was part of something bigger than himself and he intended to show her instead of telling her how much he loved her.

He clutched her arms, and stepped backward, creating space between them, and stripped off his clothing. Without speaking he undressed her, taking his time. His hands grasped her waist, and he hoisted her off the floor.

Natalie hooked her legs around Seth's waist, and his hardened shaft teased her core. He pulled her onto him, and she arched her back. "God, Seth. I love how you feel inside me."

"I love how tight you are. Will we hurt the baby?"

"No."

Seth carried her to the bed. Poised above her, he savored the connection between them.

His gyrations slow, and easy, his rhythm firm, driving her to distraction.

"Oh, Seth. God, I love you. This…this is…exquisite. It feels good. So good, don't stop, please."

"I'll do you all day long." Seth peppered kisses along her throat. His hips pumped faster but maintained a gentle firmness.

"Keep tempting me and we'll be late."

"You're a cop, you can drive faster."

Natalie gripped his shoulders. "God, Seth, please." Her hips ground against his, increasing the friction between them and heightening the anticipation.

"What do you want, Nat? Tell me." Seth brushed her lips with his, and he slowed his tempo, pausing until she squirmed beneath him.

"For the love of God, Seth, let me come now." Natalie clawed his back, her body urging him, and he plunged them into the abyss.

CHAPTER 20

H alfway to Banner Elk, North Carolina, Natalie took over driving. Her family always spent Christmas in the mountains, and she missed last year. The trip also offered the best opportunity to introduce Seth to her family.

Natalie glanced Seth's way, his head rested against the window, his eyes closed. A smile played on her mouth but faded. She needed her family's support, and for the first time, Natalie questioned their loyalty.

Unable to do anything right now, she focused on the road, negotiating the numerous twists and switchbacks, enjoying the adrenaline rush.

The stability and precision handling of the German-engineered vehicle minimized the sway but woke Seth anyway.

Trees whipping past, he straightened in his seat. "Is something wrong?" His gaze swung between Natalie's hands gripping the steering wheel and the blurred foliage streaking past.

"Nope. Damn, Seth, this thing handles like it's on rails!" Natalie said and squealed each time she entered a new turn.

"Uh, Nat. Nat. Natalie!" Seth clutched the door's armrest. His knuckles whitening, he braced himself.

"Relax." Natalie grinned.

"I should've stayed asleep. Nat!" His Cayenne zipped through the bends, hugging the lane, and rocketing out of the curves. "I didn't escape Chicago to die on a mountainside."

"Relax, baby. They taught us how to pursuit drive at the police academy."

"Uh, you're not chasing a fleeing criminal."

"No, but this if a lot more fun."

Seth stayed quiet but remained tense until they reached less curvy roads.

NATALIE PARKED behind her brother's pickup truck and faced Seth. Her hand on his thigh, she smiled. "You ready, baby?"

"I guess." Seth squeezed her hand.

"Seth, just be yourself. You're a good person."

"Am I?"

"Yes. We've all made mistakes."

"I know what they'll be thinking. You can do better than a former prostituting junkie. Your brother is a cop, and your dad is a retired cop. Come on, your dad wants better for his baby girl than someone like me." Seth's gaze held hers.

"First, if I'm happy, my dad will be too. Give people a chance, Seth. They may surprise you."

"Come on, Nat. We both live in the real world and know how others perceive people like me. Once a junkie always a junkie."

Natalie's mouth opening, she spotted her father, Carson Savage, heading their way, and swallowed her words.

The front door flew open and her niece and nephew, beaming smiles on their faces, rushed around their grandfather.

Seth stifled his trepidation and the two exited the vehicle. Natalie opened the rear door, releasing Elvis and circled the vehicle to join Seth.

"Aunt Nat." Her niece, Mattie, short for Madeline, jumped into Natalie's arms.

Josh, a year older than his sister, dropped to his knees and lavished affection on Elvis.

"Hey, guys, I want you to meet someone." Natalie disentangled herself from Mattie's grip.

Her father stopped in front of them, scrutinizing his daughter's companion and the Cayenne.

"Dad." Natalie hugged her father, and stepping away, linked her arm around Seth's. "Dad, Mattie, Josh, this is Seth."

"Hi." The pair greeted the man standing in front of them, assessing him the way children do.

"Hi." Seth smiled at the kids and extended his hand to Natalie's father. "Mr. Savage." Seth's steady tone showed no hint of his underlying anxiety.

"Seth." Carson shook the younger man's hand and gestured at the expensive SUV. "So, when did you buy this?" he asked Natalie.

"I didn't. It's Seth's." Natalie's sight journeying between her father and Seth.

Carson further scrutinized his daughter's companion, guessing his daughter was several years his elder, elevated his concern. His years of police work cultivated his ability to read people, prompting his next question after he meandered around the SUV.

"So, Seth, what do you do? A Porsche Cayenne GTS is one hell of an expensive vehicle."

"Dad." Natalie's tone held a hint of caution.

"I'm leasing it from my coach."

"Coach?"

"Seth, plays hockey for the Patriots." Natalie's arm circled Seth's waist.

"Wow, that's so cool." Josh stared wide-eyed at Seth.

"I see, and you plan on making this your career?"

"I hope so, sir."

"Let's go inside." Natalie pressed the hatch release on the key fob.

"Kids, help with the luggage." Carson gestured with his head.

"I can get it." Seth joined the kids at the rear of the SUV.

"Dad..." Natalie's hands on her hips, she huffed.

"I'm no fool. He's what, seven or eight years younger than you, and ECHL players don't make much money. How long have you been dating? You could've told us." Her father's eyes riveted on hers.

"We started dating in October, and Seth is twenty-one, and he *will* make it. Marshall Reeves wouldn't have gone...acquired him if—"

"Gone, what, Natalie?"

"Gone out on a limb for me, sir." Seth reappeared, holding their luggage. "No sense hiding anything, Nat."

"Someone better start explaining." Carson's gaze shot between his daughter and Seth, dwelling longer on her boyfriend.

"Mattie, Josh, please take the presents." Natalie's request interrupted their play with Elvis.

"Uh, sure, Aunt Nat." Josh grabbed the bags of gifts.

"Come on, Elvis." Mattie summoned the dog and disappeared inside the house.

Free of the kids, Seth on the verge of speaking, an approaching vehicle captured their attention.

"NATALIE." Katheryn Savage hopped out of the car and enveloped her daughter in a tight hug. A smile beaming across her face, she greeted Seth. "And who is this handsome fella?"

"Seth, ma'am." Seth extended his hand, and she clasped it.

"It's a pleasure, Seth." Katheryn held his.

A younger image of Carson joined the group and introduced himself. "So, my sister is still amongst the living. I'm Nick, her brother."

Seth shook Nick's outstretched hand.

"Carson, help Nick with the groceries," Katheryn said.

Seth followed Carson and Nick to the house.

"He's handsome, Nat. Tall, muscular, and those blue eyes, but young, and you're glowing with happiness." Katheryn linked her arm through Natalie's and urged her inside the house.

"He is. Seth's twenty-one, Mom. I know, I know. Please, give him a chance he's a great guy, and I love him." Natalie, erring on the side of caution, kept the baby news quiet.

"Is that all?"

"Yes, mother."

"Uh-huh."

SETH BREATHED a sigh of relief once he entered the room assigned to Natalie and himself. Her father surprised him and held off subjecting Seth to the third degree. He refused hiding or dwelling on his past. Nothing he did changed it, but he had learned from it, and it stayed a constant reminder of what he no longer wanted.

Natalie offered him hope, a future, and now a family. His early childhood was filled with deplorable examples of parenting, and he admitted, fatherhood scared him.

"Hey, baby, you, okay?" Seth's expression concerning her, Natalie crossed the room.

"Uh, yeah. I'm fine." His smile strained.

"You're a horrible liar."

"Until now, I never cared how people viewed me. Being called a junkie, a prostitute, a criminal, none of it bothered me. Honestly, it was cool. I was a tough guy and did what I wanted and got high whenever." Seth shrugged.

"Seth, everyone can change, and you took the first step on your own—"

"Only because Tre murdered that girl in front of me. Otherwise, I wouldn't have."

"But you did, and that's what matters. It sounds harsh but her death freed you from that life, so she didn't die in vain."

"I guess, but will your family see it that way? Your father already dislikes me and I'm okay with it. I'm twenty-one and leasing a hundred-thousand-dollar car from my hockey coach. Your dad's a smart man, Nat. It won't take much investigating on his part, and he'll discover the rest. Why keep it a secret?" Seth eased away from Natalie, walked to the window, and stared out, marveling at the mountains.

"How do you propose we broach the subject?" Natalie immediately regretted her tart tone.

"Hell, if I know." Seth released a deep breath and faced her "I'm sorry, Nat. I hate fighting with you. I'm worried about how their opinion of me affects your relationship with them. A family is foreign to me but in the few minutes I've been around yours, I can tell, it's special, and I'll be damned if I'm the reason you lose them."

"Seth, baby, I won't lose my relationship with my family." Natalie closed the distance between them and grasped his hands.

"You can't promise that."

"Yeah, I can. After a sit down or two with dad and Nick, they'll come around, and if not, it's their loss and they'll deal with it."

"I don't want stress between you and them. I can't be the cause, Nat. I…"

"Seth, what? Talk to me baby, please."

"It's nothing."

"No, it's something, please talk to me. Remember we agreed to always talk." Natalie coaxed, squeezing his fingers.

"The last foster family, the abusive one, hammered into my head that it was my fault my parents dumped me because I was a bad kid and I believed them. I figured it must be true, and that…I deserved the abuse. I figured eventually I'd get it right and become a good kid and it would stop, but it didn't." Seth's eyes dropped from hers.

"Oh, baby. That's not true. It wasn't your fault. None of it is your fault. You were a kid. It was their responsibility to nurture you, teach, and love you, instead they abused you." Natalie ignored the tear trickling down her cheek.

Seth stayed quiet and Natalie pulled him to her and looped her arms around him. "Seth, do you want to find out what happened to your parents?"

"Does it matter? They didn't want me."

"That's not necessarily true. Maybe they died, but it's your choice." Natalie hugged him tighter.

"So, what is there to do here? Is there anything special you do?"

"We can go hiking. Sit outside by the fire, or inside too. Christmas morning, Dad, Nick, and Josh help at the church's soup kitchen in the morning and us girls prepare Christmas dinner. You can go with the guys or stay here. No one will force you to do something you're not comfortable with."

"I'd like to help at the soup kitchen. Most times they supplied the only food I ate until Tre put me to work. Even then, I'd hit them up."

"Seth, they'll be thrilled if you go. Come on, let's go downstairs." Natalie tugged on his hand.

"Nat, help me tell your family. They have a right to know. If I make it in hockey, it'll come out sooner or later, and it's better having everything in the open now…no surprises later. Are we sharing the baby news?"

"I agree, and yes, we will. Let's see how it goes first, okay, handsome?" Natalie yanked him closer and kissed him.

"Hmm, do we have to stop?" Seth held her against him and captured her mouth.

"We have kids in the house."

"Damn, maybe we'll only have one kid."

"Oh, no. At least two, maybe five or six."

"Okay."

A smile lit Seth's face, and she swatted him on the chest. The two chuckling, they left the room, hand in hand.

ONCE THE KIDS went to bed, the family gathered in the great room. Natalie explained how she met Seth, and he revealed his past. Unsure of how they now viewed him and wanting them to have time to talk without his presence, he excused himself, Elvis on his heels.

Seth ventured onto the covered patio and wedged himself against the wooden support beam, to the right of the stone fireplace, and stared at the darkened forest. The sights and sounds of night in the mountains, more soothing than those in the city, he became lost in his thoughts.

"You might want this." Carson offered him a coat.

"Thank you. I'm used to the cold."

"Take it."

"I don't need it."

"My daughter inherited my stubbornness."

Seth accepted the coat and shrugged into its welcoming warmth, but he refused admitting it.

"I'll be honest, I'm unsure how I feel, but I respect your honesty."

"It happened. Why deny or hide it?"

"True."

Seth met Carson's gaze dead on. "I know I'm not the kind of guy you want for Natalie, but I love her. I'll do anything for her, give her everything I have. She is my whole life now, and I'd never hurt her. I can't change who I was, but I'm not that person anymore. I hope one day, you'll accept me and not hold my past against me. Excuse me."

He pushed away from the wooden beam and crossed the patio.

"Seth."

He stopped but kept his back to Carson.

"We leave at six."

This time Seth did turn. A reply unnecessary, his expression conveyed his understanding. Seth dipped his head and spun on his heel and disappeared inside.

"Hey, baby, everything okay?"

"Yeah. I'm exhausted, and you are too. Morning comes early." Seth entangled their fingers and lead them through the house.

"That's my dad's favorite coat. It was his dad's."

Seth grinned. "It's a warm coat." He stopped outside their room. "I love you, Nat."

"I love you, too, Seth. We'll have to be quiet." She grasped his hand and tugged him inside the room.

Seth and Natalie discarded their clothing in record time.

CHAPTER 21

Winter turned to spring in South Carolina and the Patriots teetered on the brink of claiming a second Kelly Cup Championship. Tyler Brennan's car accident near the arena the same night the team claimed the Cup marred last year's victory.

Seth and his teammates filing out of the locker room, Marshall halted Seth.

"I'm relying on you to keep these guys together."

"Uh, thanks, Coach, but I'm far from leadership material."

"Seth, trust me, you're exactly leadership material. These guys look up to you." Marshall slapped Seth's back.

A blush crept across Seth's face. "Thanks, Coach."

ONE MINUTE REMAINING in the game, the Patriots held a one-goal lead. The opposing team gaining possession, their goalie skated to the bench.

"Just play the puck, guys. We got this," Seth encouraged.

The seconds ticking away, Seth spotted one of the other team's defenseman glancing at the clock, and the opposing forward fired off a shot. The Patriots' goalie blocked it, but lost control and it rebounded in front of him, leaving the left side of his net wide open.

Seth skated to intercept but the rocketing puck struck his vulnerable, unprotected side and skittered out of reach.

Five seconds remained

Seth ignored his pain and muscled aside his opponent and regained possession of the puck.

Aleksander banged his stick on the ice and Seth passed him the puck.

The game buzzer sounded.

Along with his teammates, Seth dropped his stick, removed his gloves and helmet, and joined in the celebration. His throbbing ribs forgotten.

Marshall on the verge of leaving the bench, Cooper bellowing his name stopped him.

"What?" Marshall turned.

"I just received word. They want Seth in Providence."

"Really, Coop, you couldn't wait until after their celebration?"

"Sorry, it came straight from Boston. Gwyn called me personally. He wants him there ASAP, like tomorrow. Day after at the latest."

Marshall shook his head and joined his team.

THE CELEBRATION in the locker room nowhere close to winding down, Marshall pulled Seth into the hallway, a few feet from where the girlfriends and wives were gathered.

Natalie spotted the pair and excusing herself, walked to them. "Coach, everything okay?" She studied Marshall. His solemn expression gnawed at her gut. Instinct warned Marshall and Seth's discussion involved Tremaine Kingston.

"Yeah. Boston wants Seth in Providence and ASAP."

"I'm guessing that means he needs to leave now." Natalie's gaze darted between Marshall and Seth.

"I...uh...guess I need to pack."

"Let's discuss this in my office." Marshall gestured at the door.

. . .

TEN MINUTES LATER, Marshall left Natalie and Seth alone.

"Wow. Natalie, what do we do?"

Natalie pushed away from the wall. The distance closed between them. She ignored the dampness from the champagne soaking his shirt and draped her arms around his neck.

"We're going home and you're packing and heading to Rhode Island and playing in the AHL. I'm proud of you, Seth. This is a great opportunity."

"It is, but what about us, Nat? How do I do this on my own? Without you." Seth pulled away from her and paced the office.

Natalie snagged his wrist, halting his movements.

"Seth. You survived years alone on the streets. This is nothing. A stroll in the park. This is what you've dreamed of. It's one more step closer to the NHL."

"That was different. I love you, Nat. We're having a baby. It's wrong leaving you here, alone."

"Seth, baby, you are going to Providence, and who knows, Boston might be next. No, listen." Natalie raised her palm. "It's the playoffs. Once the season is finished, you'll come home, and we can figure out our next step. Right now, we need to go home and pack. It's a long drive. I wish you'd fly instead."

Silence stretched between them. Seth digesting her words until he blew out a long, slow breath.

"Come on, its late, and you'll be heading out early and need some sleep."

Marshall, awaiting them in the hallway, placed a hand on Seth's shoulder. "Seth, you'll be fine. Play your game. Be tough. Remember don't look for trouble but don't back down either, especially in the AHL. They'll try you. Brad is there. He'll help you adjust."

"Thanks, Coach."

"Good luck. Natalie, you call if you need anything, and please call Lauren, she's already talking baby shower plans."

"I will, thanks."

He waved the couple away. Marshall unlocked his phone, typed out a text, and hit send.

NATALIE PARKED Seth's vehicle and twisted in her seat, facing him. His quietness at his apartment while he packed hadn't escaped her. "What's wrong?"

"I can't leave you here alone."

"Seth, my family is here. My friends, and…Dad?"

"Dad?"

"Uh, yeah, my dad's here." Natalie pointed at the figure waiting in front of her apartment building and bolted from the SUV. Seth followed but with less enthusiasm.

"Dad, what are you doing here? What's wrong?"

"Seth is heading to Providence. With two of us driving, we'll make better time, and he can rest," Carson said, explaining his unexpected presence.

"I…" Natalie's eyes widened.

"Mr. Savage, I can't ask you to leave your family, and who'll—"

"Not your choice, Seth, and we're wasting time standing here bickering. We'll make better time driving at night."

The three entering the residence, Carson attended Elvis, allowing Natalie and Seth some private time. Upon their return Seth knelt in front of Elvis and engaged the animal in a serious discussion, outlining what he expected during his absence.

Elvis licked Seth's face and high-pawed his response.

One last ruffle of Elvis' ears, and Seth straightened and clasped Natalie's hands. Neither spoke.

"I hate being the bad guy, but the sooner we hit the road…" Carson interjected, and the trio stepped outside.

"Yeah, he's right, Seth. You need to go. I love you." Natalie threw herself against his chest.

"I love you, too." Seth wrapped his arms around her and captured her mouth.

Natalie broke the kiss. "Go." Tears threatening, she waved her hands, and disappeared inside the apartment.

"Nat."

"Come on, Seth." Carson urged, his hand on Seth's back.

His head resting on a pillow against the window, Seth checked the clock. Sleep eluded him and the first rays of daylight filtered into the SUV. Neither having spoken a word in hours.

"I appreciate this." Seth broke the quiet.

"Happy to do it."

Silence resumed. Another ten minutes passed.

"Why are you doing this? You don't like me, so why?"

Carson shot Seth a sharp look. "That's your assumption, Seth. Yes, your past concerns me, but Natalie loves you and you are the father of my grandchild."

"So, you're keeping an eye on me. Making sure I—"

"Natalie's my baby girl and I don't want her worrying. In a few months, you'll understand. The happiness of your wife and kids comes first."

"And you can keep an eye on me." Seth grinned.

"Yes, but seriously, it's a good opportunity for us to know each other better," Carson replied. "And hell, I have the time. Retirement isn't everything it's made out to be."

"You miss being a cop?"

"Maybe. No, it's…feeling useful. Needed."

"You are needed, Mr. Savage. Your family needs you."

"My family includes you now too, Seth."

Seth met his future father-in-law's astute gaze square on.

"I have no clue how to be a dad, Mr. Savage."

"First, dump the Mr. Savage. Call me Carson, or Dad, but please no more Mister." Carson's chuckle filled the vehicle.

"Ok, Carson."

"We'll stop for breakfast in another hour or so then drive a few more hours and find a hotel."

"Sounds good. I'll drive after breakfast, and you can—"

"You'll rest. I used to drive around for twelve hours per shift."

"Are we sleeping during the daytime?"

"Yup, trust me, once we hit Richmond, driving at night will be a lot easier and we'll have you at the arena for the morning skate, if you're good with that."

"Works for me. I can sleep anywhere, and I can help with the driving."

"Leave the driving to me Seth. That's what I'm here for." Carson flashed a smile Seth's way.

"Never had a chauffeur before." Seth laughed and twisted in his seat, his back resting against the side of the seat and the door.

"Don't get used to it." Carson chuckled.

The two continued conversing until they stopped for breakfast, discussing hockey and Seth's past in more depth.

SETH AND CARSON arrived in Providence, home to their parent team's American Hockey League franchise, tired, but excited.

Carson stopped at the guard gate for the players' parking, and downed his window, greeting the guard.

"Morning. Hi, Seth, welcome to Providence." Ronnie McPherson peered inside the SUV.

"Hi. You must be Ronnie." Seth extended his hand across the vehicle's cabin.

"Yup. I reserved the spot on the left." Ronnie indicated a corner space near the players' entrance. "Marshall parked there when he played here."

"Uh, thanks and thank you for putting us up."

"Beats a hotel, kid. I've seen your game footage. You'll do fine here. Keep your head up and play your game. The morning skate starts in forty minutes." Ronnie smiled, straightened, and stepped away.

Carson parked the Cayenne and helped Seth unload his equipment and the two entered the arena. Directed to the coach's office, Seth knocked on the open door.

"Coach Picciotto?"

The man standing in front of a white board, marker in hand, spun around.

"Hi. I'm Seth Doyle."

"Seth, come on in. I wasn't expecting you until later this afternoon."

"I, we, made good time. My girlfriend's father came with me. He drove most of the way. I'm ready to suit up, Coach."

Coach Picciotto assessed his newest defenseman, filling the doorway, and smiled. The marker placed on the board's lip, he circled the desk and extended his hand.

"Then let's get you situated and introduced to the team. You already know Brad," Coach Picciotto said, adding a hello to Carson on their way to the equipment room.

"Seth, this is Jim Kiser, our equipment manager. Jim. Seth Doyle. He's skating this morning and suiting up for tomorrow's game. Seth, I'll see you on the ice. Carson, you're welcome to hang around and watch practice."

"Thanks, but I'll go take our luggage to Ronnie's and come back," Carson said.

"We'll get him there. You look like you need some rest," Picciotto said.

SETH'S ARMS full of compression shorts, t-shirts, socks, and other non-uniform team garments, Jim led him to the dressing room, and he changed out of his street clothes. The two did a quick tour of the facility, ending at the locker room.

Jim pointed at an equipment stall and said, "Hope you're okay with number eighty-eight."

"Uh, yeah. It's an honor. Thank you." Seth fingered the jersey hanging on its peg. Marshall wore the number when he played here and in Boston.

HIS TEAMMATES already on the ice, Seth wasted no time outfitting himself in his protective gear and uniform. The laces on his skates tied, he gathered his gloves, helmet and stick and Jim escorted Seth to the ice and he skated out, joining his new teammates at center ice.

Brad Myurzz's smile and welcoming nod eased Seth's tension, but the hairs on his neck prickling, he scanned the squad. His gaze landed on Russ Thackeray.

"We have a new defenseman joining us. Seth Doyle." Coach Picciotto addressed his team and appointed his line combinations for practice.

"You're aware there's bad blood between Doyle and Thackeray," Kevin Murphy, the team's assistant coach stated.

"They're teammates now, good test on both their parts."

"But in our final series? With the Cup on the line?"

"You've seen the game footage of Doyle, the kid's a force to reckon with." Coach Picciotto smiled at his assistant coach.

"We'll find out soon enough. The first line? You're sure?"

"We need his size."

THE PRACTICE CONCLUDING, Seth's side ached but he ignored it. He'd ice it later at Ronnie's.

"Doyle." Thackeray tossed a water bottle at Seth.

"Thanks." Seth caught it and doused his face with a liberal amount of the liquid and drank the rest.

Showered, changed, and despite a few wrong turns, Seth found the door to the players' parking lot. Thackeray shouted his name and he stopped.

"How are the ribs?"

"Excuse me?"

"Your ribs. Have they been checked out?" Genuine concerned filled Thackeray's voice.

"I'm fine. Why do you care?"

"Regardless of our past, we're teammates now."

Seth studied Thackeray for a long thirty seconds. "Yeah, I guess we are, and the ribs are fine."

"I'm sure they are, kid." Thackeray slapped Seth's shoulder and walked out, the door closing behind him.

Seth shoved it open. "Hey, wait up."

Thackeray stopped midway across the parking lot and waited. Once Seth reached him, Russ said, "There's a great wings place nearby."

CHAPTER 22

Seth stepped onto the ice for his first game at the American Hockey League level, one tier beneath the NHL. His expression unreadable.

He spoke with Natalie for an hour prior to the game and he continued repeating her encouraging words. Her soothing voice calmed his nerves.

The linesman dropped the puck for the starting face-off and Seth focused on the game.

Seth collected two hits on his first shift. Both substantial and hindered the Laval Hogs' offensive runs.

Last night during dinner, Thackeray briefed Seth on their counterparts' style of play and supplied the numbers and names of their opponents' fastest forwards and their more aggressive defensemen. Seth stored the information for future use.

HIS NEXT TWO shifts progressed the same. The Hogs centered their offensive attack on Seth's side of the ice expecting to take advantage of his youth and inexperience.

At the halfway mark, Providence scored, notching the first goal of the game. Seth's defensive play facilitated his teammates' success and gained him another first at this level, an assist.

Seven minutes remaining in the period and Seth leveled another hit on Laval's leading forward. Seth grinned at his opponent's obvious frustration and skated away from the boards.

"Keep grinning. I'll knock those pearly chicklets right out of your fucking mouth," a Laval Hogs' defenseman chirped.

"Bring it." Seth glared at the player hounding him.

His opponent rammed his stick into Seth's side, catching the bruised area. Seth masked the pain and jostled the man.

"You think you can take me?" His nemesis pushed him a second time.

"Yup." Seth shoved the man with extra force and his opponent stumbled.

A linesman stepped in and separated the two, keeping them from exchanging blows.

Providence regained control of the puck, and Seth's teammates raced it into their offensive zone. He pushed off his skates and away from the nuisance Hogs player.

Two strides from crossing the center ice red line, Seth's vision blurred, and a pain tore at the corner of his right eye. Instinct brought his hand upward. Warmth dripped into his eye, and he slowed his speed.

"Just a starter, rookie." The defenseman shouldered Seth and skated off.

Blood dripping to the ice dictated he exit the rink and he skated for the bench. He nodded at Thackeray standing at his assailants feet.

Seth glared at the man and said, "Game on, later," and the pair left the ice together.

Two minutes into the third period, Seth upheld his earlier taunt, and exchanged blows with the tormentor. Seth won the one-sided bout and entered the penalty box.

Coach Picciotto cocked his head at his assistant coach.

"Still worried?"

PROVIDENCE DOMINATED the first three games. A win tonight secured them the Calder Cup Championship. Seth arrived at the arena earlier than necessary and phoned Natalie from his Cayenne.

"Hey, Nat."

Her golden tones spread warmth through him the moment she answered. He missed her, and despite loving hockey, he counted the days until the season ended.

"Hey, baby."

The two chatted until a rapping on Seth's window interrupted. Seth said his goodbyes and exited the vehicle.

"You okay, kid?"

"Yeah, thanks, Russ. Natalie and I always talk before I go inside. I sure wish she was here." Seth locked the vehicle and the two crossed the parking lot.

"Hockey's tough on a relationship, kid. You have a picture?"

"Uh, yeah. She sent me this one earlier. We're expecting a baby in August." Seth tapped at the photos on his phone

"I remember her. She's a cop, right? Good-looking woman, and congratulations. It's none of my business, but what happened that day?"

"It's a long story."

"Then give me the short version." Russ held open the entrance door.

Inside, Seth rolled his shirt sleeves above his elbows. Seth adept at hiding the fading traces of needle marks, he bent his arms and revealed them.

"During my first pro year, a teammate convinced me steroids were the quickest and best way to enhance my game, and it became a problem. Hence, why I'll stay stuck at the ECHL level with the occasional jaunt here in the AHL during playoffs."

"I mainlined heroin, snorted coke, and popped pills," Seth said. His new friend's revelation prompted Seth sharing a shortened version of his past and resulting in his and Tremaine's ultimate encounter that day.

"Wow. I'm lost for words. Except, I'm glad you escaped and are making something of yourself. That's a huge accomplishment. Proud of you, kid." Russ squeezed Seth's shoulder and smiled.

"Thanks."

"Come on. We've a game to win. It'll be nice ending my career with a championship."

"You're quitting?"

"More, retiring. I'm not going anywhere. I stopped fooling myself years ago. It's time I move on. I'm tired of being the next team's goon."

"What will you do?"

"Hell, if I know. Coach somewhere, maybe. I'll figure it out. But you, kid. You're going far."

"Everyone keeps telling me that. If I do, I'll need a personal trainer and skating partner."

"Next season, you'll have no problem affording the best out there."

"That may be true, but I want someone who understands hockey. Think about it?"

"I will, but first we're winning this fucking championship."

The conversation switched to hockey and the two changed out of their dress clothing. Coach Picciotto summoning Seth halted the friends' conversation, and he shot a questioning look at Russ. His teammate shrugged.

Seth hastened to his coach.

"I preferred telling you this later, but I have no choice."

"Okay." Seth drew out the word.

"Regardless of tonight's outcome, you're expected in Boston in the morning. I begged them to let you play with us tonight. Straight after the game, you hightail it to Beantown. The defenseman paired on the top line with Colin Montoya has a concussion."

"Wow, okay. I need to make a few—"

"Carson's packing your personal belongings. We'll have your gear packed at end of the game and you can head straight to Boston. There's a hotel room waiting near the arena. Go, call your girlfriend, but, Seth, keep your head in the game tonight. There's no guarantee you'll see ice time in the big league." Coach Picciotto pushed away from his desk and approached his defenseman.

"I understand, Coach, and thanks for everything here." The two shook hands.

"Focus on the game. They're out for blood."

"I got this, Coach."

Back inside the dressing room, Seth called Natalie.

Providence claiming the American Hockey League championship title, winning the Calder Cup, Seth became the first player to win championships at the ECHL and AHL levels in his first professional season.

An hour later, Seth and Carson headed to their next destination, Boston.

Boston playing in the final series for the Stanley Cup, and tied at one game apiece, Seth was in a position of becoming the only first-year pro player to win a championship at each of the three professional levels within the same franchise. He hadn't skated in the requisite number of games to qualify for rookie status in any league other than the ECHL.

Statistics of no concern to hims, but Seth's stats, and quick ascension from the franchise's lowest tier to its top one, brought him immediate media attention. His lack of history in the game fueled their interest. In Charleston, Marshall and his teammates guided him through interviews, and Natalie's presence bolstered his self-confidence.

On the outskirts of Boston, Seth turned his thoughts to helping

Carson locate their lodging. This time, a hotel became their home. Checked into their room, Seth called Natalie. The late hour shortened their conversation.

The call disconnected, Seth stared out the window, overlooking Boston's home arena.

"Rest, please. It's been a long day and a tough game. Your morning skate is at ten." Carson said.

"I miss Nat."

"She's there, Seth." Carson tapped the center of Seth's chest. "She's always right there."

"I know, I just really miss her."

"Love has that affect, but distance can also make a relationship stronger."

Seth lingered near the window for a few more minutes. Stripped out of his clothing, he climbed into one of the beds, and slept.

Images of Natalie invaded his dreams. He woke in the morning longing for her. A thousand thoughts raced through his mind. His past, and its effect on the way others perceived him, at the forefront of his thoughts and anxiety. Unlike before, now he cared.

Carson showering, Seth rose and prowled the room. For the past two years he resisted the seductive call of needing a good high.

Sweat peppered his body. His hands trembled and his heart raced. Seth pulled on his clothes and rushed from the hotel room. Inside the elevator he pressed himself against the wall. He stepped out on the first floor, colliding with a solid object, and excused himself.

"Seth Doyle?"

"Uh, yeah." Seth eyed the stranger, his features familiar but his identity elusive.

"Colin Montoya. I was on my way up…are you okay?"

"Uh, hi. Yeah, I'm fine." Seth clasped Montoya's hand and pushed forth a smile.

"Let's talk over breakfast."

"Sure." Seth accompanied his new team's captain, and thankful for his timely arrival.

The two crossed the hotel lobby and entering the restaurant, Colin directed Seth to a corner table.

Natalie rising from the booth stopped Seth dead in his tracks, and his breath lodged in his throat. Her smile drew him into her arms.

"Nat? Natalie." Seth swung her in a full circle, set her down, and kissed her. He ignored the interested observers.

"Hi, baby," Natalie said once she broke free of Seth's long, passionate kiss. She stayed in his arms but nodded at Colin. "You should say thank you to Colin."

Seth dipped his head and met Colin's amused grin. "Thank you."

"You're welcome. You two enjoy breakfast. Seth, I'll see you in an hour. Natalie." Colin grinned, shook Seth's hand, and left.

"How did you get here? I thought—"

"Seth, shut up and kiss me again. Our food is getting cold, and you need a good breakfast." Natalie linked her arms around his neck and kissed him.

BREAKFAST FINISHED, Seth escorted Natalie upstairs. Her flight having drained her, he insisted she rest instead of accompanying him to the morning skate.

Perched on the edge of the bed, Seth stroked Natalie's growing baby bump. His eyes lingered on her belly.

"Seth?"

"Huh."

"Are you okay?" Her hand covered his. "You need to go."

"I know. I'm so happy you're here. I've missed you, Nat. I panicked this morning. I...I...wanted...you know."

"Baby, it's okay. It'll happen. You'll always be battling the cravings, and stress adds to the challenge. This is a huge step. It's your opportunity to show them what you can do."

"I know, but there's no guarantee I'll play."

"True, but I have a good feeling, Seth. It's obvious they believe you have the skill to play at this level."

"They brought me up because of an injury."

"True, and there are other defensemen they could've chosen, but they picked you. Show them they made the right choice. I'll be at tomorrow's game, and whether you dress or not, enjoy the experience." Natalie swung her legs off the bed, bringing her alongside Seth, and leaned against him.

"I love you, Nat." Seth tipped his forehead against hers.

"I love you, too, Seth." Natalie pressed a searing kiss to his lips.

CHAPTER 23

Surprise greeted Seth on game day, dressing and playing. He clocked limited minutes, but he made his presence known, and his ice time increased with each subsequent game. Despite Boston losing the next two games, the team led the series three games to two.

A VICTORY TONIGHT concluded the series and handed the team back-to-back Stanley Cup Championships…no pressure.

Coach Pike entered the locker room, and the team's chatter hushed. A long minute passed, and he addressed his players.

"We all know what's at stake tonight. Play our game…and have fun. This is our night. Colin," Coach Pike said.

Their team captain stood. "Okay, boys, we're taking this game. We're starting with our top line forwards Lakovic, Jarrell, and Brennan." Colin paused and his gaze shifted from Tyler to Seth, seated alongside his former Patriots teammate. "Doyle you're paired with me."

Seth straightened and kept his jaw from dropping. The start unexpected.

"Congrats, you earned it." A broad grin on his face, Tyler elbowed Seth.

The game buzzer echoed into the room and the players filed past Colin. He issued words of encouragement and fist-bumped each one making their way to the ice.

The starters waiting in the tunnel for their introductions, Colin faced Seth.

"You nervous kid?"

"Nope."

"Good, they'll come at us hard tonight. Let's show them who's boss out there and give them hell." Colin chest bumped Seth.

"Glad you're with us, Seth." The goalie, JR Rapp, tapped his stick against Seth's leg.

"Thanks. I got you tonight." Seth smiled and entered the ice at the announcement of his name. The darkened arena and strobing lights prevented him from spotting Natalie in the suite designated for players' families. Her presence surrounded him and bolstered his confidence.

Seth's heart hammered in his chest during the national anthem. The music faded and he skated into position on the left side of their defensive blue line, Colin to his far right. A glance in Colin's direction, and a slight nod of his head, he acknowledged his teammate's unspoken message, and focused on the task at hand, winning.

Two minutes into the second period, Sean Jarrell scored, tying the game at two. Five minutes later Dallas scored the go-ahead goal..

The minutes ticking away, tension filled the arena and the noise from the home crowd was deafening.

Ninety seconds to go and Dallas snagged the puck on a bad bounce off the boards on Brett Lakovic's pass to Tyler Brennan near their offensive blue line. A Dallas two-on-one ensued and Colin, caught deep in their offensive zone, left Seth closest to their defensive blue line.

Seth drew on his street smarts and focused on the forward on his side of the ice, Nashville's leading scorer, Marshall's words ringing in his head.

Play one player on breakaways and let your goalie focus on the other.

One eye on the lead scorer and the other on the forward controlling the puck, Seth anticipated his opponent taking advantage of his inexperience and feigned indecision on which player to defend against. The ploy worked and the forward passed the puck.

The opposing forward fired off a one-timer shot, and Seth skated into the path of the puck. The rubber disk struck his injured side and he hit the ice, landing on the puck. His delay in rising triggered a stoppage of play, burning precious seconds off the game clock.

Tyler, having gained possession of the puck, skated hard toward their offensive zone. Ten seconds left in regulation, his former Patriots teammate netted his second goal of the game, forcing overtime.

HALFWAY INTO THE second twenty-minute overtime a steady throbbing centered in Seth's side and intensified each shift. He ignored it.

Neither team scoring and five minutes remaining, Seth gritted his teeth and positioned himself for the face-off occurring in Boston's defensive zone due to an icing call. Boston unable to change players, Dallas took advantage of being allowed a line change and initiated one..

His eyes swung to Colin positioned alongside him, their hands on their knees, catching their breath, the team captain opened his mouth, but Seth spoke first.

"I'm fine."

"Bullshit." Colin cracked a grin, and both readied themselves for the face-off.

The puck dropped, and the physicality to gain possession escalated.

Colin placing a heavy hit on a Dallas player, Seth battled another opponent for possession. Despite several jabs to his side, he played through the pain and freed the puck. Brett snagged it and along with Sean and Tyler, worked it into their offensive zone.

Tyler, having joined Boston in November, shot on goal. The loud smack resounded throughout the arena and the puck slammed into the netting behind Dallas' goalie.

The thunderous cheers from supporters drowned out the final buzzer.

Seth joined his teammates in a third championship celebration. This time Seth enjoyed the occasion instead of rushing away to hit the road.

"Doyle." Colin hugged Seth. "Have your side checked."

"Later."

Colin, shaking his head, skated off. Seth locating the family suite, blew Natalie a kiss.

"Save it for the bedroom, Doyle." Brett bear-hugged him.

The traditional end-of-the-game handshake completed, and the formal on-ice ceremony finished, the team carried their victorious elation to the locker room.

Out of his uniform and protective gear, but doused in champagne, Seth left the locker room. A few wrong turns and an arena worker directing him, he located the family lounge.

"Congratulations, baby." Natalie launched herself into Seth's arms.

"Thanks. I'm glad you're here, sharing this with me." He pulled her close, and kissed her, and not a simple one.

Seth lingered until Natalie shooed him away and he returned to his teammates.

"HEY, EVERYONE, LISTEN UP." Colin's voice boomed through the room, and silence prevailed. "After each victory we present our Marathon Award."

Colin reached into his stall and removed a bronze sneaker.

"Seth." Colin handed his line mate the trophy.

A barrage of cheers erupted, and the revelry continued.

THE POST-GAME INTERVIEWS FINISHED, his side checked out, Seth showered, dressed, and returned to the family lounge. He located Natalie in a deep conversation with Casey Taylor and Heidi Jarrell.

Natalie's back facing him, he smiled at Casey and Heidi, holding his finger to his lips, and sneaking up behind her, he tapped between her shoulder blades.

"Hey, baby."

"Hey. Hi, Casey, Heidi." Seth grinned at the two Boston police officers. Both welcomed Natalie with open arms after meeting her at dinner that first day they were in town.

Casey and Heidi excused themselves, leaving Seth and Natalie alone.

"How is your side?" Natalie tipped her head.

"It hurts. Broke a rib." Seth looped one arm around Natalie, and the pair headed out of the arena.

Seth opened the passenger door of his Cayenne and helped Natalie inside. His hand on the door, he stopped.

"Seth."

"Yeah."

"I love you."

"I love you, too, Nat, and this little one, too." Seth rested a hand on Natalie's baby bump and bracing himself on the car door he kissed her.

EPILOGUE

The wail of a baby bounced off the walls of the delivery room. Seth, transfixed with joy, stared at the tiny infant nestled on Natalie's chest.

"You have a son." The nurse smiled at the new parents.

"Hey, little fella." Seth clasped his son's tiny hand, awestruck at how it disappeared into his larger one. He grazed his lips across Natalie's temple. "He's beautiful."

"Handsome, like his dad." Natalie's weary eyes swung from her son to his father.

Without warning, Natalie's face paled and a pained groan increased to a deafening yell, prompting the nurse and Natalie's OB doctor, already at the door, to return.

"Doc!" Panic consumed Seth. "Do something. What's wrong?"

"Mr. Doyle, let me have the baby." The nurse elbowed Seth aside.

"Seth...ooooh, fuck." Natalie pressed her head into the pillow.

Torn between losing sight of his son and Natalie's obvious distress, Seth vacillated. His common sense overrode his agitation. The baby in good hands, Natalie's distress became the greater concern.

"Uh, Ms. Savage, you're having twins." The doctor issued a stream of commands and prepared for the birth of another baby.

"T-twins?" Seth sank into a chair, his mouth hanging open.

"Yup. Okay, Natalie. You got this. This one will be much easier."

"How the hell did we not know this." Natalie grimaced once the next contraction hit.

"It happens." The doctor chuckled and smiled.

"Wrong answer, doc." Natalie ground her teeth.

"It's okay, Nat. I'm here."

"Christ, it…this is your fault." Natalie glared at Seth.

"Actually, it's both our—"

"Shut the fuck up, Seth."

Another shriek followed Natalie's command.

NATALIE CRADLING HER DAUGHTER, she peered at Seth holding their son.

"I'm sorry about earlier." Her smile weak, and she yawned.

"It's okay. I know how you can make up for it." Seth waggled his eyebrows and flashed her a devilish smile.

"You're bad."

"To the bone, baby." Seth edged closer and brushed his mouth to hers. He placed a soft kiss on top of his daughter's head.

Exhausted, Natalie nodded off.

Seth slid his arm around her and drew her and their daughter closer.

He marveled at his new family.

His family.

ABOUT THE AUTHOR

Despite first putting pen to paper in 1990, it took another thirteen years and a TV police drama before I was truly motivated to trust my instincts and give writing a proper go. I'm hoping one day to finish those first rough drafts!

Already an avid reader, thanks to my dad's encouragement, my favorite genres are historical and Regency era romances, and my ultimate favorites are anything hockey, ancient Rome, and the American Civil War.

Married to a police officer for twenty-two years, I am also a sucker for romances involving first responders. Other than reading and writing, I love to travel, with Italy at the top of my list. My love affair with this most ancient of countries culminated in 2011 when, after the passing of my mother-in-law, I was offered her airline ticket and journeyed to Italy with members of my husband's family. Visiting Rome and Pompeii sparked a deeper fascination that has seen me return several times and inspired at least three of my books.

When not traveling, reading, immersing myself in anything hockey-related, or writing, I spend time with my husband and our two minia-ture dachshunds, Bailey and Stuie (celebrities in their own rights, but that's a whole other story), enjoying the beach, and catching up with friends in our local car club. Most importantly, I supported my husband during his law enforcement career, which wasn't an easy endeavor.

Please check out my Facebook page – Josie Naclerio - Author for the latest on upcoming releases. I hope you come to love my everyday heroes as much as I do. Enjoy! https://www.facebook.com/Josie-Nacleri-Author-2192405504134478

f

OTHER BOOKS BY JOSIE NACLERIO

Current releases available on Amazon

The Carabinieri Series
Love in the Ruins – Book 1
Italian Love – Book 2
Carabinieri Love – Book 3

The Hockey Series
Skating on Love – Book 1
Love's Penalty – Book 2
Blue Line Love – Book 3

A Military Charity Anthology
One Day at a Time – featuring A Sniper's Love

Destination Collaboration Series
Stealing the Mountie's Love

Future Releases
The Carabinieri Special Forces Series
Royal Love – Book 1
Love's Special Forces – Book 2
A Sniper's Love – Book 3

The Carabinieri Series' Finale
Presidential Love

LOVE'S PENALTY
Book 2
https://books2read.com/LovesPenalty

Instalove...or lust? Instinctive evasion. Trust tested. Tragedy present and past.

A Caribbean cruise seemed a small consolation to Canadian-born star winger Brett Lakovic following his team's crushing defeat in the final game of the Stanley Cup Playoffs. Until he crashes into a beautiful blonde on the running track…

Injured in a tragic house fire, Boston police officer, Casey Taylor, is a reluctant passenger on the same cruise, but the seductive magic of the Caribbean is providing the perfect remedy.

An unexpected encounter leads to a sizzling romance, but Casey fears her occupation will scare off the smoking-hot pro hockey player.

Brett's attraction is instantaneous but is it enough to overcome her deception?

Neither is aware of the danger lurking in the shadows. A ghost from Brett's past is hell-bent on destroying his future.

In a twist to rival the drama of the playoffs, Brett and Casey's newfound love faces the ultimate penalty.

BLUE LINE LOVE
Book 3
https://books2read.com/BlueLineLove

Against the odds. Second chances.
Is love enough?

Sean Jarrell, Boston's rising-star center, is on his way to success. His hefty new contract and playing the sport he loves provides him the stability his abusive childhood lacked. Nothing, absolutely nothing, will stand in Sean's way.

Determined to put the devastating line-of-duty death of her fiancé behind her, Boston police officer, Heidi Gutro, is ready to move on. She is making strides, but tragedy strikes again resulting in the death of another officer and her best friend getting shot. Deciding relationships are too hard in her line of work, Heidi closes her heart.

A chance meeting in a hospital elevator tests their resolve…will it bring Sean and Heidi love? Or more heartache?

THE CARABINIERI SERIES

LOVE IN THE RUINS
Book 1
https://Books2read.com/LoveInTheRuins

Dreams fulfilled as love blooms. A deranged adversary resurfaces. Past meets present.

Archaeologist, Rebecca Walker has been granted the job of a lifetime, to work in the ruins of Pompeii, her dream since she first visited the ancient site. A week later she arrives in the town, excited for this new chapter in her life.

Weary of the bloodshed after years of fighting terrorist insurgents in foreign lands, Gian Caravello returns to Pompeii planning to finish his career with the Carabinieri in his hometown.

A forgotten backpack and an unwelcome phone call bring the two together. Their instant and undeniable attraction deepens with every spare moment spent together but is their happiness doomed before it ever starts. Two thousand years ago Vesuvius destroyed Pompeii. Now a terrible danger lurks, threatening the couple, and a ghost from Gian's past is intent on wreaking revenge.

In a place where ancient and modern collide can Gian and Rebecca survive, or will their love end up in ruins?

ITALIAN LOVE
Book 2
https://books2read.com/Italian-Love

Choices with consequences. Lurking danger.
International intrigue.

What appears to be an innocent encounter in a hotel lobby in Dubai, sets off a chain reaction with dire consequences.

Returning to Italy, from Australia, with her best friend, Stefania, Abbey Capelli isn't interested in romance, or even a fling, despite the gentleman's impeccable clothes, dynamic good looks, and obvious interest.

Alika Kostidis has other ideas and tracks his quarry to Florence only to find another vying for Abbey's heart.

Harboring guilt and grief following the death of someone close to him, Federico Valente, Stefania's older brother, is resolved never to fall in love again. It's not worth the pain. His conviction is turned upside down when his sister sends him a photo of Abbey. Her image sets his blood on fire, and when he meets her, his fate is sealed.

Although flattered by Alika's attentions, Abbey's heart belonged to a certain, tall, devastatingly handsome Carabiniere before they ever met.

Losing isn't an option for Alika.

Head over heels in love, Abbey and Federico have no idea all is not as it seems in fair Florence. Prowling beneath the surface, a malicious evil is poised to destroy their happily ever after.

CARABINIERI LOVE
Book 3
https://books2read.com/CarabinieriLove

Reluctant celebrity. Childhood Dreams…or nightmares.
Smoke and Mirrors.

Thrust into the spotlight since birth, Riccardo Mariani, once Italy's golden boy, walked away from it all to join the Carabinieri, Italy's military police.

Italy's most famous actress, Sophia Pignataro, always dreamed of kissing Italy's golden boy under the ruined Portico d'Ottavia, nestled in the heart of the Eternal City.

Fate brings the two together, sparking a hot steamy romance the moment they meet, only to be extinguished when Sophia discovers Riccardo's real identity.

Can their love overcome the lies and secrets surrounding Riccardo, or will Sophia's *Carabinieri Love* crumble like the relics of ancient Rome's?

DESTINATION ROMANCE COLLABORATION SERIES

STEALING THE MOUNTIE'S LOVE
Canada
https://books2read.com/Stealing-the-Mounties-Love
https://buff.ly/3bPMRZb

An International Romance. Web of Intrigue.
Testing Fate

A simple visit to retrieve a family heirloom becomes a race against time to save more than just a stolen treasure amid the breathtaking landscape of the Canadian Rocky Mountains.

When Braden Lauzon, Royal Canadian Mounted Police K-9 officer, reaches out to his childhood friend in England, Rose Chapel, regarding the discovery of her family's psalter, neither anticipates what followed.

Recovering from a near-fatal shooting, Braden prepares to return to work, never imagining his sworn oath to protect and serve his community would include Rose, his childhood crush.

All it takes is a letter, and Rose flies to Calgary. Her family's psalter safe in hand, her rekindled lost love sparks something far more enduring.

When Rose's return to England is thwarted by a brazen robbery, her lover is tasked with hunting down the thieves who will stop at nothing to achieve their objective, including murder, in this page-turning novel blending a steamy romance with the drama of police action.

Can Braden save the Chapels' prized possession, or will he find himself fighting for his life again?

Made in the USA
Middletown, DE
11 March 2023